WITHDRAWN

Can You Get There from Here?

SOUTHWEST LIFE AND LETTERS

A series designed to publish outstanding new
fiction and nonfiction about Texas and the
American Southwest and to present classic
works of the region in handsome new editions.

GENERAL EDITORS: Kathryn Lang, Southern
Methodist University Press; Tom Pilkington,
Tarleton State University.

Can You Get There from Here?

Stories by

Donley Watt

Southern Methodist University Press

Dallas

These stories are works of fiction. Names, characters, places, and incidents are either the product of the author's imagination or are used fictitiously.

Requests for permission to reproduce material from this work should be sent to:
Rights and Permissions
Southern Methodist University Press
Box 415
Dallas, Texas 75275

Some of the stories in this collection appeared first in other publications: "Not Just Another Waltz" in *High Plains Literary Review;* "Waiting for a Good Day to Leave" in *1990 Roberts Writing Awards Annual;* "Ducks" in *Tucson Weekly;* "Flying" in *Writers Forum;* "The Way the Big World Is" in *New Texas '92;* "The Man Who Talked to Houses" in *CutBank;* "The Way Things Happen" in *Concho River Review;* "Can You Get There from Here" and "A High Place" in *Southwestern American Literature.*

Library of Congress Cataloging-in-Publication Data

Watt, Donley.
    Can you get there from here? : stories / by Donley Watt. — 1st ed.
        p.   cm. — (Southwest life and letters)
    ISBN 0-87074-376-7. — ISBN 0-87074-377-5 (paper)
    I. Title. II. Series.
PS3573.A8585C36   1994
813'.54 — dc20   94-5095

Cover art and design by Barbara Whitehead

Printed in the United States of America on acid-free paper
10 9 8 7 6 5 4 3 2 1

For Donnalyn, Celia, and Martin
for Kathy and Mike
and always for Lynn

Contents

In the Mood

Wᴵᴸˢᴼᴺ liked to take Sandy for a ride in the country on her day off. Since the real estate office out on the lake had closed, every day was his day off. Riding around made him feel good, like he was moving on in life and not just sitting in Sandy's house waiting for her to get home. His pickup was three years old and had covered some rough ground, but it had air and a good radio and Wilson felt the Ford would take him anywhere he wanted to go.

Sandy had gone to a costume-party fund raiser for the hospital the night before and as they headed out of town, she told stories that Wilson only half heard. He had stayed home and sipped on bourbon and studied the atlas. Washington or Oregon—it was down to that now. He had to get out of Texas, you couldn't sell anything to anybody in Texas.

"Robert Hinkle, you know him, from the bank. He came as a nerd." Sandy had lived in Crosby all her life and at one time, before the oil boom in the early eighties, knew everyone in town. "We nearly died, his hair was parted in the middle and he wore these thick glasses, and what was funny, he didn't look so different."

Her voice was high and excited and Wilson liked her that way. Or at least he had at first. That little-girl freshness is what attracted him to Sandy. She worked in the County Clerk's office, in the courthouse, stamping documents when they came in, copying them, then filing them in the right books—deeds, deeds of trust, whatever. Wilson knew it was necessary work and that Sandy liked it, but eight to five all week was not for him. Since the bust she had been cut back to four days a week, but they still got by.

Her office cluttered one bright corner of the third floor. From there you could see the little downtown square, the Palace Drug Store and the Bluebonnet Cafe, and, from across the high-ceilinged room, you could look down on what was left of the Liberty Theater. It had burned a couple of years before and was still black and gutted, its screen puffed and crazed like antique glass. Wilson didn't go up there much, but when he did he always felt that the world grew a little bigger.

As he listened to Sandy he drove west, past acres of asphalt that surrounded a Wal-Mart, past the Sonic and then the high school with its Crosby Cougars Stadium. A block off to his right he saw the Oak View Apartments, a place he had hung his hat until his job folded and he moved in with Sandy. It bothered him, being almost forty and out of work, but he still had a little money put aside and helped with the house payments, so no one was hurt. The arrangement annoyed Sandy's mother, who ever since made a big deal about calling before she came over, and then yakked with Sandy as if Wilson was in another county and not lying low in the next room.

The land on past the edge of town was open. It lay flat as a platter, with rutted lanes leading to a house or barn here and there and an oil derrick or two still scattered in the fields of cotton and soybeans.

"And Betty Grobe came dressed as a little Dutch girl with a sign around her neck. Oh, and she carried a stuffed goose —I don't know where she got it. The sign said something like 'If Gretel had not been a goose-girl she might have had more friends.'" Sandy laughed and looked at Wilson, who forced a smile and tilted his straw hat back on his head. She put her hand on his leg, her fingernails glossy red against his blue jeans. "I guess you had to be there. You know, for it to be funny."

"Goose-girl," Wilson said. "Yeah, that's great." Jesus H. Christ, he thought, what the hell am I doing here? Portland or Seattle, it was between those now. All that green, the smell of pines, some mountains on weekends. And a job for sure, a good one. He could sell anything as long as it wasn't in Texas. You couldn't sell anything here, he thought again and frowned.

He looked out at the flat fields, the black soil that turned to gumbo when rain blew up from the gulf. On those days, which in this part of East Texas happened often, you could see tow trucks and dozers pulling rigs in and out of the fields. Or you could before the bust. Now when it rained, the farmers and what few roughnecks were left gathered in the Bluebonnet Cafe. Wilson tried it a couple of times but quickly had enough talk. As he told Sandy, "Down and lower, that's all there is. The price of oil, real estate, you name it. Cattle? The pits. Maybe the Oilers? What a laugh."

"This is Raymond's weekend—with the kids, you know," Sandy said. While she talked she wound a loose thread back around a button on her blouse. "Sweetheart, are you listening?"

In his mind Wilson rode a ferry that was plowing across Puget Sound, but hid his surprise at being jolted back. He stared intently as a white-breasted hawk beat its way above a lone tree.

"Did you see that hawk?" he asked. "The power—Jesus." And he shook his head in amazement.

Sandy bent down and half-tried to see the bird, but couldn't. "Sweetheart," she said again, and this time Wilson nodded and quickly glanced her way. "I have an idea. Why don't we go to Houston Saturday? Raymond will have the kids. You can look for a job during the day and we can stay at that Howard Johnson's near Astroworld, where we stayed before. Just the two of us. We can pick the kids up on Sunday afternoon and be back before dark."

Sandy liked Raymond better now that she'd divorced him, it seemed to Wilson. The past six weeks, ever since he had been laid off, it was always "Raymond this, Raymond that." Wilson thought he was a real asshole. Raymond packed it off to Houston after they split and had moved in with a woman who looked ten years older. He paid Sandy fifty bucks a month for the two kids and took them every third weekend. Kim and B.J. were a handful, and in the two years Wilson had known Sandy he had seen Kim, who was twelve, get the upper hand. She was older than B.J. by two years and was pretty like Sandy, with fair skin and golden hair that had just enough curl to turn up on the ends. He thought Kim was a little too smart for her own good, a little too much like Raymond, but Sandy couldn't see it.

Wilson tapped the steering wheel with his fingers and looked off to the left where a line of scrub oaks clung to a fence. He lifted his finger and nodded as he met another pickup going into Crosby. They'd had some good times in Houston, in that Howard Johnson's; some good times, and not just there. "A weekend out of here sounds great, really it does," he said, "but a job in Houston? You can forget that."

"Raymond got a job. I don't know how, but he has a good job. Houston's not all that bad." She tossed her head once and ran a finger across the pickup's dash, making some design in the dust that Wilson couldn't make out. Her hand was smooth, but her fingers were short and a little pudgy. Wilson looked over at her.

"Managing a goddamn Pizza Hut's not a job. Not in my book, anyhow." Shit on Raymond, Wilson thought. Then he asked, almost spit the words, "If he's so damned smart, why'd you leave him?"

Sandy flushed a little. "That's not what I meant," she said. "Oh, just forget it." She folded her arms and stared out the side window. Yeah, two years and he still couldn't read her. Sometimes he wished she would fight back. It would be easier to leave that way. That's what happened with Marsha, the last woman he tangled with. They had one final ball-bustin' fight and he was gone.

They got quiet for a while. The pastures were grazed down to nothing. Grass couldn't grow in August; even with rain it was too hot. A hell of a place to be, Wilson thought. He leaned forward and his shirt peeled off the plastic seat. The road was straight and from there it was only a couple of miles to the county line. He would feel better later. They would eat some barbecue and down a couple of beers and maybe things would lighten up. They both stared down the highway and Wilson watched as the illusion of a pool gleamed on the asphalt in front of them. He knew Sandy was watching it, too, and he figured that she thought he would say something, but he didn't. The pickup was silent except for the hum of the V-8 and a soft puffing sound that escaped from the rusted tailpipe.

They passed a series of white rectangular signs hung from fences along both sides of the road. Stenciled in red and blue, the words danced with fuzziness: REPENT NOW and ETERNITY WHERE? and JESUS CARES.

Sandy studied them, or maybe she was still thinking about what he'd said. He couldn't tell. He'd sworn never to live with another woman. Not after the last one he'd had, not after Marsha. Pain and pleasure, pain and pleasure. He was worse than a junkie living with her. Shreveport had been good to him; he made a little money, had some good times. But Marsha. She reminded him of the old nursery rhyme "When she was good she was very, very good," but, Jeesus! "when she was bad . . ."

"Who do you think puts those signs up?" Sandy asked. "Did you see those religious signs, sweetheart?" She undid her seat belt and turned toward Wilson. She put one hand on his shoulder and grinned. "I bet I know who didn't," she said, and pinched him and laughed.

Wilson laughed, too. Don't be a fool, he thought. She's so damned easy, just love her a little, take it slow, something good will show up. "You're wrong," he said, with a sly, sideways look. "What do you think I do all day? Gonna get me a TV show next—the Wilson Dolan Good Times Hour." Sandy's face was aglow again. "Brothers and sisters, send your dollars to Dolan." His voice was full and deep and he knew it, he had used it before to convince, to sell. At one time the world was going to be his with that voice and his looks, but for the most part he'd left the looks back down the road a piece.

"You old liar, you." Sandy giggled and slid over next to him. She gave him a kiss on the cheek, an exaggerated smack, and then sat back. "Now apologize," she said with a false pout. "You were mean—now apologize."

Wilson ignored her except to reach over and squeeze her thigh. Then he pointed to a handpainted sign, red letters on a white piece of plyboard that had faded to gray. "This is where I've been wanting to go. Supposed to be good."

IN THE MOOD — REAL PIT BBQ
This is It

Wilson read it aloud and laughed. "I hope that's right," he said, and repeated "This is It" over again slowly as if those three words were the first words of some favorite song.

A gravel driveway led up to a frame building with a screened-in porch attached to one side. On the other side a metal roof sloped away and protected a blackened pit. A circle of smoke drifted uncertainly from there and slowly curled its way free over the roof where it lifted out of sight. A handmade sign tilted down above the open door.

HOURS and MENU
I barbeque what I want when I'm here
and I'm here when I'm
IN THE MOOD

Wilson ran his fingers across his thin black hair, slapped his jeans a couple of times with his hat, and they stepped inside. No one was there and Sandy took Wilson's hand. A long table filled most of the rectangular room. It was covered with a red-and-white-checked oilcloth that was stapled down. A basket of yellow onions sat in the center of the table, flanked by a loaf of white bread and a jar of jalapeños. A grease-coated ceiling fan turned lazily above it all and kept the flies from settling in any one spot.

"Just a minute, folks." The voice came from a small adjoining room where, through a screen door, Wilson could see the glow that flashed from a television set. Then he heard applause and laughter and "God almighty, that's right!" A man wearing a grimy white apron emerged from the dim room. "They sure get some smart suckers on them shows," he said. "Won a goddamn Camaro. Wouldn't have one myself." He looked Wilson in the eye, then noticed Sandy and took a step or two back and nodded, eyeing her up and down.

"Thought we'd try some of your barbecue," Wilson said. "You've never had barbecue till you've had Quentin Bandy's," the man said as he moved past them and out toward the pit. Off to the side, next to the stacks of mesquite, Wilson saw a pile of boards broken up for kindling. Even split in half longways, he could make out parts of a "Repent Now" and a "John 3:16" tilted across the pile. "Now here's some real brisket," Bandy said as he plunged a two-pronged fork into a slab of beef.

Bandy carved thick slices of meat and placed them fanlike on two lengths of butcher paper. Then he drizzled and dabbed some thick sauce all over. It was the color of mashed persimmons and ran to the four corners of the paper. Bandy wrapped the remaining meat in foil and hustled it back to the pit. Wilson watched him move and figured he was the kind of fellow you wouldn't have to jump-start to get moving.

"Let's eat in here," Wilson said, and he led Sandy into a dark narrow room with a bar along one side. A jukebox glowed against one wall and a Pearl Beer sign with a tireless waterfall gleamed softly from another. Above the bar hung a shotgun, painted white, with a sign that read "For Formal Weddings." Sandy pointed to the sign and giggled, but Wilson didn't laugh.

Wilson was right. After a couple of beers he did feel better and things lightened up. Bandy pulled up a chair and straddled it backwards, his hairy arms propped on the chair's top rung. They ate and drank and listened to his stories. He had lost his barbecue place in Angelo when his wife left him; she didn't like the smoky way he smelled all the time and his fondness for Wild Turkey.

"She got religion. Church of the Nazarene. Spent more time there than with me," he said. Bandy looked thoughtful and a little sad. He watched Sandy glide over to feed the jukebox and then turned back to Wilson and said, "Not that I gave a shit."

A fellow wandered in and then back out with a barbecue sandwich and a six-pack—what Bandy called a Texas seven-course meal. He brought two more Pearls to their table and said to Wilson, "You need more beer—help yourself. Just leave your empties on the table." Bandy gave him a slap on the back and disappeared through a curtained doorway that led to what Wilson guessed was the kitchen. He glimpsed Sandy as she glided back his way, but kept his eyes on the Pearl as it sweated on the table.

"Let's dance. Sweetheart, you want to?" Sandy stood back from Wilson and turned slowly, her arms outstretched, her eyes half-closed. Crystal Gayle caressed the room with "Don't It Make My Brown Eyes Blue."

A little beer does her some good, Wilson thought, loosens her up. She turned once and beneath her blouse he saw a little roll of flesh that bulged where her bra was too tight across her ribs. He hadn't noticed before but now he could see that everything was too tight, in a strain: her jeans, wrinkled at the waist, and the pink blouse that stretched across her breasts. He could see her pale skin where it buttoned.

"Sweetheart, come on, let's dance." She leaned down and put her arms around his neck. He could smell beer and onions battling with her perfume. "I've gotta take a leak," he said and pulled away.

"Well, I'll just have to dance by myself," she said with false haughtiness and then laughed as Wilson ambled off.

He liked the hell out of that song, reminded him of nights with Marsha, her eyes brown and deep, not like Sandy's, which were blue and all on the surface with everything bouncing off.

When he came back a man was at the table with Sandy. He was a tall fellow with hair that curled all over and was silver moving on to gray.

"Curtis Sitterle," he said, half rising out of his chair and offering Wilson his hand. "Hope you don't mind," and he motioned to Sandy. "I've known this little woman for years," and he laughed, "more than I like to remember."

"Sweetheart, you remember Curtis," Sandy said. "He helped with Lake View Estates when it first opened. Or maybe that was before you worked there." And she looked at Wilson in a puzzled sort of way.

Wilson remembered Sitterle's name. He had lost the details but recalled something about him being the project manager and pocketing double commissions. But it was before Wilson got there and he knew how small towns were, how gossip and lies spread faster than the truth, so didn't let it bother him.

"Curtis is doing really great in Houston. Buying, what is it, Curtis?" Sandy asked.

"Well, it's not that great, but for a down market, we're doing quite well, I guess." He had a well-trimmed beard and wore a sport coat with silver flecks that sparkled even in the low light. Wilson didn't like that way of talking—this "down market" bullshit, this "quite well." And if he's so damned smart what's he doing here on Wednesday afternoon, he thought, but kept his mouth shut.

"Here's a cold beer, sweetheart. Curtis bought us a beer." Sandy was beaming. Wilson watched while she looked up at the other man. She was pretty when she turned her head to the side that way. He felt like a stranger watching her, like he had pulled her photograph out of an old album that had been lost. And a feeling he had forgotten washed over him, but he didn't show a thing.

"Sandy tells me you're between jobs, that you know real estate." Sitterle leaned forward while he talked. He was a big man, older than Wilson by five or more years. "We might could use someone else. We're chasing these repos down and it's a real job. Of course, dealing with the FHA's no easy trick either. But it pays off. If you know what you're doing, that is."

"That sounds wonderful! Doesn't it, sweetheart?" Sandy asked. "I thought of doing real estate myself once," she said and looked kind of dreamy.

"What happened to the music?" Wilson asked. He dug into his jeans and brought out three quarters. He pushed them across the table to Sandy and said, "Anything but that damned brown-eyes-blue song. You must have played it a dozen times."

"Here, I'll help you," Sitterle said and pushed his chair

back. "I've dropped a few quarters in those boxes before," and he laughed easily.

Wilson watched as the two of them walked away. Sitterle was a foot taller than Sandy and she stretched as high as she could while they talked. At the jukebox she playfully bumped him to one side with a swing of her hips and Sitterle limped around in a circle and laughed.

Bandy appeared from the back room wiping his hands on his apron. He stopped behind the bar and watched Sandy and Sitterle at the jukebox. Then he came over to where Wilson sat slouched in his chair with one boot propped on the edge of the table and his hat pulled low over his forehead. Bandy had two cold Pearls and handed one to Wilson. "This one's on me." Wilson looked up and nodded his thanks. Bandy cleared the empties off the table and disappeared behind the curtain again. The beer was cold and felt good to Wilson's throat, but the buzz had slipped away after the first three or four and left him with a dullness, a heaviness, that more beer couldn't cure. Not today, anyway.

"She's quite a gal." Sitterle was back. "Yessir, quite a gal you've got there." He lit a cigarette. It was long and thin. A woman's smoke, Wilson thought.

"Sandy says you may be in Houston Saturday. Come by and let's talk." He shoved a card across the table and Wilson slid it into his shirt pocket without a glance.

"I doubt I'll be there. No telling where I'll be Saturday." Even with the beers, Wilson could hear the flint in his own words.

"You can't be choosy nowadays," Sitterle said. "But that's your business."

"Sure is," Wilson said, and both men were quiet. "Waltz Across Texas" started up on the jukebox and Wilson stared at the waterfall clock on the wall. It was four-twenty.

"I love to waltz, I *love* it, I *love* it." Sandy was back and waltzing around the table. Dancing usually didn't mean much to Wilson, just another way to use his charm. But he wanted to dance then with Sandy, like he had a thousand times before with an endless trail of other women. He felt heavy in the chair, though, and didn't move. She looked at Wilson for a moment as he stared at the waterfall, watching it flow off the wall. Then she grabbed Sitterle by the hand and pulled him into the middle of the floor. He gave Wilson a silly grin and a shrug as Sandy whirled him off.

Bandy wandered back through the room and wiped a couple of tables down. He twirled the towel until it was tight and snapped it at a fly, then glanced over at Wilson and gave him a sympathetic wink.

Wilson watched awhile. He muttered a soft "son of a bitch" under his breath. Sitterle *could* dance and Sandy followed smoothly, the heels of her shoes clicking on the wooden floor. She turned gracefully, laughing and out of breath, and Wilson saw the way she danced and knew it came from wanting to be there, from needing to move. He understood.

When the waltz started again, Wilson walked stiffly across the room and out the door. Through the glare he saw Bandy poking more mesquite in one end of the pit, coming up for air out of the smoke and shaking his head.

The pickup was hot so Wilson rolled the windows down and sat with both doors open. He flipped through the pocket and pulled out a map, but it was of Texas and that didn't do him any good. He knew how to get out of Texas. He read a two-for-one pizza ad that he found stuck behind a visor, then precisely folded it as small as he could.

"Not leavin', are you?" Bandy asked. Wilson hadn't heard him walk up, but had smelled the smoke.

"I owe you for some beers, don't I?" Wilson asked and reached for his billfold.

Bandy pointed back to his place. "The other fellow, he paid already." He looked at Wilson a minute and asked again. "You're not leavin', are you?" Wilson stared down the highway and didn't answer; he didn't know how to answer.

"You know," Bandy said, his voice soft and even, "what I said about my old lady was true. But she was a good woman, at least good enough for me." And he laughed. "I'm damned sure no great catch."

Wilson looked up at him and sure enough, he probably wasn't a great catch. He had a little too much of everything he didn't need, including years. But he worked hard and seemed sincere and so was probably honest, and those weren't the worst traits a man could have.

"Your woman's all right," Bandy said, looking Wilson right in the eye. "She's young and pretty. And she likes to dance. You can't blame her for that. She your wife?" he asked, and Wilson shook his head. "Well, I need to get back to that damned barbecue," Bandy said, and he looked back toward the pit, shading his eyes from the sun. He took a step or two away and turned as if to say something else, but didn't, and shuffled off.

Wilson sat for a while and followed the smoke as it rose and circled and blended with the soft clouds. Then he strode to the building and felt Bandy watching as he opened the door. The music swirled around Wilson as he stood in the open doorway, his arms folded, the bright sun at his back. He watched as Sandy danced across the floor with Sitterle. He waited for that moment when she would turn and see his silhouette, dark and framed against the light.

Not Just Another Waltz

OKAY, I say, but before I begin this story, you need to know the ground rules. You follow them or I show you the door. Is that clear? Julie doesn't say a thing, just puts both thumbs under her hair and lifts it, waves it a minute in the steamy air, and lets it fall back, straight and light.

She's still standing inside the door and I'm pacing, not that I'm nervous, but so she can see I mean business. I stop and point my finger at her. You came here asking; you let me do the talking, from when I start to when I stop. No interrupting, no getting angry or crying. If that happens, it's adios. You got that? She nods and says okay, but I see she doesn't like it.

I motion to the table and watch her while she takes in my trailer and then eases into a chair. She's small like Ray, her daddy, but doesn't favor him, her eyes blue and wide-set with eyebrows painted in a shade dark for her light hair. She's wearing jeans a size too tight and a T-shirt with TIJUANA angled across the front. She must favor her mama, Ray's ex, who I never met, but who Ray would talk about when a night stretched long enough, a woman Ray said was some kind of a looker.

It's afternoon and the trailer's hot, but you can't hear a thing with the a/c rattling and roaring along. So the unit's off and before you know it we're both sweating and sipping Lone Stars with the door open. If you can't stand the heat, I think . . . and hope she can't, hope she'll leave.

Julie didn't hear about her daddy being killed for a few months, but that's her fault for running off to California and not staying in touch. Many a night the last year or two I'd be at Ray's apartment when he tried to trace her. We'd down a few cold ones and he'd dial Sacramento and San Jose and Santa Cruz. A night for the S's, he'd say and laugh. Ray wanted to find Julie, to know if his only kid was okay. But I'd ask what you gonna say when you find her? and he'd just grin and say hell if I know. Sometimes I think Ray didn't want to find her at all. I always thought it was funny, the way Ray never said a word about Julie when she lived across town, but soon as she left he started worrying. Sometimes I think when he drank beer he liked to get on the phone and talk and didn't give a damn who was on the other end. Ray was like that. He'd see an ad in the paper that said "Talk to Japan for 95 cents a minute," and next thing you know he'd have the international operator dialing Japanese numbers until someone answered. Then I'd time him, watching my Timex all the way, giving him the cut sign at fifty-eight seconds and he'd hang up. Ninety-five cents worth of Japanese gibberish and a couple of laughs for sure. But I won't tell Julie. She's not here for that.

When she came to the door she said something about wanting to hear the story of how Ray died, hoping she could reconnect—that's her word, not mine—reconnect with her daddy. You were his best friend, weren't you? she asked, and I nodded and let her in.

Now the hard part starts, and I watch her real close, reminding her again how she agreed to listen, to hear me out. I settle into a chair at the dinette, straight across from her. I wipe my hands down the legs of my jeans and plant my elbows square on the yellow speckled top. I lean forward and look her right in the eye. "Ray was my best friend and I killed him," I say, and then settle back and wait a minute, hoping she'll hit me or spit on me or anything as long as she'll stomp out right after. But she sits there, without a twitch or a blink, her eyes like little ponds of blue ice. I heard something like that, she says, then. And I want to hear more. So I go on.

Not that I'm a cold-blooded murderer or meant to do it, I say, but I killed him just the same. A man could blame it on lots of things and I'll admit right off I've tried them all. But five months is long enough to invent reasons, especially wrong-headed ones. Some people say if it hadn't been for this, if it hadn't been for that, then blah, blah, blah. That's bullshit, pure and simple.

Being out of work for six months can make a man act crazy, can push him to the edge. And there wasn't diddly-squat for work around Houston then, not in the oil patch, anyway. And that's where Ray and me belonged, putting in twelve-hour shifts out on the rigs, six, seven days a week.

I lean back in the chair and feel my whole body sag. Julie, I ask, you don't really want to hear this, do you? Pulling it out of me's not gonna bring your daddy back. And you think this is easy? You think I don't miss Ray? What do you want? To punish me? Hell, I'll get you a two-by-four; it'd be a lot easier. And anyway, I say, where were *you* when Ray was around? Why the hell didn't you care then?

Okay, okay, she says. So I wasn't a girl scout. Just take it easy. Tell me what happened, so I can see it, like in a movie. Then I'll have it up here, and she taps the side of her head with a finger, where it's mine and I can turn it off and turn it on, like a projector. The way it is now it just flickers, with lines all through it, first this and then that. All out of my control. You understand?

Yeah, I think so. But you need to understand, too. How it was before with me and Ray when times were good. I stop a minute, thinking about back then, just a few months ago. She seems to be in no hurry, and I'm damn sure not, so I go to the kitchen and bring back another couple of Stars. Her bottle's only half empty, but she hands it to me and takes the cold one. I say you want to know about your daddy, you have to know about me. She tosses her head to one side and says who's complaining. Then she folds her arms under her breasts, like she's got all day, and I catch myself staring at the way her breasts swell out against her T-shirt. Then she turns and looks at the little TV across the room as if some soap is on. I push my cap back on my head before going on and watch her, the way she's peeling the beer label off with one orange fingernail, not even looking. Ray was forty-two, and I figure she must be twenty-one, twenty-two. She's quiet like him.

You married? I ask.

Been married, she says. Men are jerks.

Not your daddy, I say. Ray wasn't no jerk.

How could I know? she says, her face all clouded up like a thunderstorm's blown in.

You listen and I'll tell you, I say, feeling an edge creep into my voice.

With a twirl of her hand she says, who's stopping you? I'm listening. Keep talking. So I do.

At the time some folks blamed what happened to Ray on Z, a woman I knew back then. Z claimed to be a gypsy, but she said lots of things, so who knows. Now Z could be blamed for a lot, but I can't put a heavy rap like Ray's death on her. Not that she liked him; she didn't. Z was jealous, I guess. She knew how much I thought of old Ray and wanted me and everything I had just for herself. She was always grasping and fighting whatever she came up against. By the time she hooked up with me her life had been one long slide, and not one of those super-smooth water slides, either.

I tilt my chair back against the wall and pull out a pack of Camels. I tap one halfway out and reach it over to Julie, but she shakes her head and takes another sip of beer. I watch her a minute before I start up again, see the smoothness under her arm when she lifts the bottle. Yeah, I say, Z sure could be full of fire. Once she said to Ray, right in the middle of a nice dinner, the three of us at the Red Lobster, she said Ray, your idea of formal is drinking beer from a glass. Then she tossed her red hair back from her eyes and grinned at Ray just like she was the devil itself.

Let me tell you what else, I say, then you'll start to get the picture. Another time we were sitting right here, and I point around the room, and Ray was going on about his idea of what he and I could do if we paid down on a little workover rig he'd run across and hit the road together. He was figuring it all out on the back of a beer coaster when Z grabbed it and sailed it clean through the kitchen. She said Ray, you're a redneck dumbass; you couldn't tell a red wiggler from a French tickler. I laugh just thinking about it, but Julie doesn't.

She's studying hard on the beer label, trying to peel it off in one piece. I shake my head and say uh-uh, Z was wrong again. Your daddy wasn't no dumbass, I'll tell you that much. Z could say things like that right to Ray's face and he'd just grin. I guess it was up to me to take up for him, but dammit, I never did.

Funny, we were on a workover rig, me and your daddy, just like the one he wanted us to buy, the day it happened. A few years before you wouldn't have caught me around one of those little rigs, but being half-broke takes the proud out of a man. A workover rig, you know, they're the ones that jackknife on the back of a truck and go around those muddy little fields, just big enough to barely pull the pipe out of the hole. So you pull the pipe and stack it and rework the pump or clean out the hole. Everything's predictable. That's not for me. Give me a big rig, let me work tower and swing those drill pipe in place and watch those long suckers spin and lock together and feel that raw power and the weight pushing down, not knowing if you'll hit a pocket of gas that could damn near suck the whole mother under or blow you off the top. That's for me, getting good money for living with all that energy and just enough risk.

Did Daddy like that? Julie asks. Working the big rigs like you?

Just like me, I say, and for the first time I see a little smile on her thin lips, making tiny wrinkles at the corners of her eyes. She's been listening close, and all at once I see what she's doing, why she's here, what she meant about making a connection.

Your daddy was one of a kind. A lot of men wouldn't have put up with Z like Ray, but he did it for me, I guess. He must have figured from watching us in action, then hearing me bitch and moan half the time about her, that he'd been there before Z and he'd be there after she was gone.

You want another beer, I ask, and she says, why not, so I go to the kitchen, get the beers and stretch a minute. What if I had a daughter like this, I wonder. What if it was me dead and Ray talking to her. What would he say? What does she need to know? How would he treat her?

I come back in the room and she's standing by the window, looking out on the acres of trailers around us. A light breeze stirs the ends of her hair. Her pink T-shirt is soaked and sticks to her back. No bra, just like I suspected. Then she sits back down and says go on ahead. I start to say I'm sorry to ramble so much, but she cuts me off.

You told anyone before? she asks.

Nobody that matters, I say.

And I matter, she says.

If you're Ray's daughter, you have to, I reckon.

Then go on ahead, she says, I figure I need to hear this.

Well, at the time I felt pretty beat up, stayed in bed for the two days before the funeral. At first I swore off booze, blaming the beer for what happened, but by that first night it took more than just a little Old Fitz to help me sleep.

Does it still? she asks.

Should it?

That depends, she says.

On what?

What kind of man you are.

You know, I say, before you called this morning I thought I'd put it behind me. At least for the most part.

She's quiet for a minute and I'm hoping she might let me off the hook, just back off from the whole thing. She runs the beer bottle across her forehead, leaving a little path of drops, never taking her eyes off me.

Why were you and Daddy friends? she asks.

Why? I never thought about why. Working together, I guess.

Working together doesn't make friends, she says. Not necessarily.

No, I guess not. But it's different working on a rig, how you get close to someone, get to be pals like me and Ray did. Understand, you can't talk for the noise, even when you take a break or stop long enough to eat, the rig never stops. So all you can do is grunt and gesture and cuss and laugh. You work like this for a couple of years, and then count the hours you've spent together back and forth to work in one or the other's pickup. And I stop to figure it out. Let's see, three hundred days times two-and-a-half or three hours; divide that by twenty-four and multiply by two years. Now that's a lot of time. You have a hangover, your buddy covers for you; he gets the flu you take him a bottle of whiskey. You get so on payday, your money's his, and his is yours. You don't worry who got the last beer or whose quarters fed the pool table or the jukebox or who bought eggs and hash browns at two in the morning. When you're pals you know it'll even out.

I look at Julie and the ice in her eyes is melting a little. Her hair is straight and long and I wonder how she'd look with it fixed, curled on the ends. Maybe she'd like a permanent or something. The least I could do for old Ray.

You beginning to get the picture, I ask, beginning to see how it was with me and your daddy?

I'm seeing it better, she says.

Of course, when women get involved it's different. Women are always the exception. But when you understand each other, you know the other's territory, just like you have some kind of radar that gives off a special kind of blip and then you know to stay away. That's what happened the night I first met Z at the Country Tavern. You know where it is? You been there?

Uh-uh. Not there, she says, and shakes her head.

Well, it's a place back off old Highway 90, hid down in a grove of pines, on your left if you're headed for Beaumont, which is all the more reason to stop. Unless you know that neck of the woods you'd zip right by on the interstate and end up in some let's-pretend place like Gilley's. The Country Tavern has a monster of a black barbecue pit out to one side and on Saturdays it's stacked to the top with pork ribs. You want something else, you go somewhere else. You want barbecued ribs you go to the Country Tavern on Saturday night. Now two-step or waltz I can do, and any fool who knows his left foot from his right can do the cotton-eyed Joe, but the band that night played something they called progressive country swing, trying to recapture Bob Wills or who cares else from the thirties, and whatever that rhythm is pretty much keeps me on the sidelines. I'm old enough to know it's one thing to dance and another to make a fool of yourself. Z didn't know this, or else didn't give a damn, and Ray and I both watched her mis-stepping along with first this fellow and then the next. Now we both had our eyes on her; I could tell and I figure he could, too, but neither of us said a word.

Julie wipes at her face with a napkin, dabbing the sweat above her lip.

Then I say, Julie, does this bother you? Talking about your daddy this way. Neither one of us was angels, you know.

She says, no, or maybe a little, but angel or not, he was still my daddy. Closing my ears to it now won't ever change that.

You've got a good head on your shoulders, I say. Just like Ray. I can sure as hell tell that.

I swear that she blushes then, and I look away so as not to embarrass her. The sun's a little lower and the air through the door begins to cool down. Julie gets up and moves to the kitchen, pulling at the legs of her jeans. Another beer? she asks, just like she's right at home, and I say sure.

She reminds me of Ray some, the way she has a mind of her own, and I wonder what ever happened to keep them apart.

Can we sit over there? she asks, and hands me a beer, nodding toward the sofa that sags against the wall. That chair's so damned hard, she says, and rubs her butt with her free hand. She nests herself into one corner of the sofa, folding her legs up under her, and I take the other end, sliding down a little so I can prop my boots on a chair.

Now let's see, I say, where was I? Oh, yeah, at the Country Tavern. Then Z sat down across the way with her girlfriend, neither one of them girls, however; even in the half-light you could tell that. But, as I later found out, Z didn't give a damn whether she was twenty-five or thirty-five. Things like age made no difference whatsoever to her. She was always perfectly happy to be just what she was at any given time. That might sound like a wonderful way to be, and it was for her, but it'll wear you down if you have to live with it.

Anyway, Z sat there all breathless and laughing, tossing that red hair of hers, and I know what happens next sounds like so much bullshit, like something that happens only on a TV show, but I swear it's the truth. The swing boys were taking a break and "Waltz Across Texas" started up on the jukebox, and she looked right over at me, like it was a dare, tilting her head back, like she was saying okay, I'm game, how about you? Now right here's where this radar thing between me and Ray comes in. It's like I gave off this signal; maybe cavemen did the same thing to keep from killing each other off, fighting over women. Anyway it's a signal that I could feel going out and Ray picked it up like he was a satellite dish, and the next thing I knew it was waltzing time in the Country Tavern.

Of course, other signals take over then, the kind Z and I had, the kind that lead you, blip, blip, blip, where you want to go. Then later, at other times, the signal goes in a high pitch, like an alarm, deet, deet, deet, but you, like the fool you are, are still hearing blip, blip, blip. That's the secret of life. Hearing the signals for what they are.

You fell in love? Julie asks. With this Z woman?

Crazy in love. Or just crazy. Who knows?

Julie laughs a little and with one finger wipes down the outside of her beer bottle and smooths the cool drops across her face.

Y'all had some good times, didn't you, she says, you and Daddy.

We're both quiet a minute before I answer. Yeah, we did, I say, and feel my lips go dry and my eyes a little wet. And all of a sudden I'm tired of what I'm saying and what I've done and what I've been—and even what I am. But there's no way out now but to keep going.

Let me finish this up, I say. Ray's Ford was in the shop so we caught a ride out to the rig that morning, and Z picks us up in my pickup just before dark. I hand Ray a six-pack and set the cooler in the back. We're headed back to town; spent one long-ass day on that little pissant of a rig. Z's driving, and I'm next to her and Ray's riding shotgun. The windows are down, wind whipping through the cab, dark enough out for bugs to go splat, splat, splat, smearing up the windshield. Z's bitching about how dirty we are, saying "How did I get stuck with a couple of mud dobbers like you?" and saying how somebody'll have to clean up the pickup before we go out. We always went out on Fridays.

Ray and I ignore her. We crawl west back along the interstate. A couple of lanes are closed off and we move no more than five or six miles in half an hour. Z's antsy to get home, for me to get cleaned up so we can hit the Country Tavern before happy hour shuts down. I say to her, to hell with happy hour. We've worked our way through one six-pack and I know there's another iced down in the back. At first I say Z, pull over, Ray'll jump out and grab the beer, but she won't. Just shakes her head and keeps driving. She doesn't drive with her hand, but with her wrist hung over the top of the wheel, her fingers flashing, all nails and rings. I say, hell Ray, you can run faster than she can drive. We're not going more than twenty at the most, and I reach over like I'm about to open his door, but he laughs and grabs my arm. Then Z says, Ray you get out of this pickup and you'll walk your butt home, by god. Now I'm starting to get pissed. I say, Z, me and Ray worked our asses off all day, it's Friday and goddammit you can stop for ten seconds for us to grab a beer. About then, Z got it in her head to pass a whole string of cars on the right and whips off on the shoulder, dust flying everywhere. I say, you're crazier'n hell, woman. We're rocking along on the shoulder and she sees an opening up ahead and floorboards the Chevy. All this time your daddy's been sipping away, staying a half beer behind me, but now he puts his arm out to brace himself against the dash and he cusses as beer foams out over his hand.

Then I don't know what comes over me. I say, this'll slow you down, goddammit, and I reach over and in one motion, like I'd practiced it all my life, I turn the key off, pull it out and with a big whoop hand it to Ray.

Julie sinks back on the sofa then and says, oh shit, but I ignore her.

I grabbed that key just like it was another time and I was fifteen again and steering wheels didn't lock. Then it's all a blur. We angle off to the right, crash through a barrier, Z screaming and cussing, jerking at the frozen wheel, trying to brake that truck down from damn near sixty, and then we slide into a bar ditch and everything flips a couple of times.

I lean back. Julie's white, glowing in the half-light of the trailer.

Well, that's how it happened, I say. I'm here and Ray died with my pickup keys in his hand.

I stand up and move over to the window. You know, sometimes I watch TV and think I see Ray, sitting alone on a stage in a chair, staring straight into the camera, sort of like Yul Brynner did. He has his finger pointing right at the camera and says, when you see this I'll already be dead, but let me warn you, don't hang around with that fellow, he's dangerous to your health. And I can feel his finger poking me in the chest.

Julie comes up beside me and we're both quiet. From the little rise my trailer's on, the whole world looks like it's filled with a million other trailers. I must have never really looked, known there were so many. They go on forever, all square and wide and silver and white, shining like so many stalled covered wagons, too many to pull into a circle.

Julie puts her hand on my arm and squeezes it hard. You're a decent son of a bitch, she says, like she was reading it out of a dictionary, soft and steady. You know that, don't you?

I keep staring out the window, but in a minute I shake my head and say, no, but it helps if you think so.

She moves to the door and I say, hey, don't go, not yet.

Why? she asks, and I know why, feel the answer in a whole mix of ways. I want to hold her and comfort her and have her hold me and comfort me. I want to love her like the daughter I never had. I want to love her like I loved Ray.

But there's more, I know, and I hate myself for thinking it. I want to be young again, to have just met Julie somewhere nice, not in a bar, not in a beat-up trailer like this, and I want to smell her hair, clean and fresh and curled on just the ends while she lies next to me.

She's still at the door, waiting for me to say something, and I think, if I'm quiet and still, she'll stay here, she'll have to wait forever. And I freeze, not moving a muscle, not blinking, straining to hold everything in place.

Waiting for a
Good Day to Leave

"I FIRST meet this gal, you know," Lonnie says, "I think now here's a nice woman. Real nice, you know, real smooth."

"Yeah," I say. "I know what you mean."

I'm listening—Lonnie *is* my brother—but I look around the room, then glance at a clock behind the bar. Six-thirty. I need to go.

"We have a drink—I buy, of course," he says. "Sure," I say.

"We talk a little. She leans my way, puts her hand on my leg, just for a minute though. Real class, you know."

"Uhmm," I say, and roll a piece of ice around in my mouth.

"Her mind though, it's like a bowling alley."

"A bowling alley?" I ask.

He leans toward me then and almost whispers. "I'm telling you, her mind's like a goddamn bowling alley."

I don't say anything, just stare at the cubes weeping at the bottom of my glass and listen.

"You know how you walk into a bowling alley and it's all bright, all lit up, with a little snack bar in the back and those solid balls and shiny lanes?"

Lonnie raises two stubby fingers in the air, holds them until the bartender notices, then looks at me. I shake my head, remembering the time, remembering that I need to head for home. So Lonnie says "Make it one" and gets back to his story.

"But then the clatter starts and pins scatter and fall—all but a spare one or two. And there those two pins sit, the one and the five, and they won't stop rocking. The whole damn rest of the place is business as usual but for those two pins, and they just won't stop rockin'."

Lonnie tests the fresh drink and shakes his head. "That's her mind, everything hunky-dory but for a couple of pins."

"Women are strange," I say, and I think about Josie, how she's not strange. Maybe that's the problem—Josie's not strange at all.

"Yeah," Lonnie says, "they damn sure are strange."

"I'm taking off," I say, draining the last of my bourbon. I would like to stay, to tell Lonnie that I'm leaving Josie, but I'm not sure when, so I figure it'll wait. It's October already and I couldn't do it now, not with Danny's birthday coming up. Thirteen's a big one. Anyway, what's a couple more months after fifteen years? By December, though. Plenty of time to tell Lonnie.

"Hey, it's early," Lonnie says and grabs my arm. "Astros'll be on at eight," and he glances across the room at the giant screen. "And about this woman, let me tell you, that's not all, not by a long shot."

"What else?" I ask.

Lonnie has a great sense of timing, so for a minute he stirs his drink with his pinkie and doesn't look up. Then he starts talking again, this time like he's thinking hard, his head cocked to one side.

"They're always regular at first—am I right?" he asks.

"At first," I say.

Lonnie laughs and rolls up his sleeves, covering up the mother-of-pearl snaps.

"Tell me 'bout it," he says, then continues. "Well, like I say, she's regular in every way, except for her looks and her bowling alley brain. She has a body that won't wait. You'd never know it the way she dresses. You've seen her in here— yeah, loose blouses, nice tailored jackets, never give her a second look. No flash at all until you get her you know where." Lonnie's eyes light up in the dim room.

"Yeah, know what you mean," I say, but I've all but forgotten that feeling, that spark that lights up a man's eyes.

Then Lonnie leans over close. "But then, right out of the blue, just when things are getting interesting, she says, 'I feel like a dark astronaut, like a dark astronaut.' That's what she says, over and over again."

He stops to watch a couple of women come in the door, laughing, one of them carrying a stuffed giraffe and a balloon that says "30!". Then he turns back to me. "Four A. fuckin' M. in the morning, and she's lying in my bed, moaning about being a dark astronaut. She's not dark at all, you know.

"So I turn on the lamp, then get up to take a leak and leave the bathroom light on. By then she's sitting up in bed, naked except for a half slip she's pulled up to here," and he holds one hand up chest high. "She's swaying back and forth and carrying on, and there on the wall I can see her shadow making this double image . . . Jesus," he says, and shakes his head.

"She'd drunk a bunch, I bet," I say.

"Two margaritas. That's all. No salt. Said salt would clog your arteries or something. So she knows what she's doing? A salad and two margaritas and next thing you know she's swaying in the middle of my bed like a goddamn cobra."

"No shit," I say.

"Then she says 'Gravity has failed' and 'I'll sail away' and repeats it a couple of times like a chant, and she starts shaking so I grab her hand. Stiff as a damned one-by-four.

"Well, it's beginning to scare the bejesus out of me. I pull my jeans on and go to the kitchen and make some coffee, wondering how bad things have to get to call a hot line number or something, and thinkin', shit, I don't want no trouble—not with a strange broad, for Christ's sake. But by the time I'm back she's gone. I never heard a thing. Like she sure enough sailed out the window."

"Well, I'll be damned," I say, shaking my head. Then I ask, "You ever see her again?"

"All the fuckin' time," he says, again in a whisper, and looks around the bar. "Never another word about that night though, like everything's copacetic." He straightens up then and pulls a Pall Mall from a soft pack and taps it on the bar. A grin crosses his face. "She don't know it yet, but she's met her match. Yeah, old Lonnie wasn't born yesterday."

"I'm taking off," I say, and stand, reaching for my billfold.

A woman walks by, then turns and stops next to Lonnie. She leans around to glimpse his face. "Lonnie. Is that you?" Then she slides onto a stool next to him, holding her drink with both hands, her back to the bar. She's not particularly attractive, but more than just plain.

"Sheila," Lonnie says. "Hey, what's cookin'?" He gives her a little peck on the cheek and turns to introduce us. "Sheila, this is my brother Jackie."

I nod. "Well," I say, glancing at my watch even though I can't read it in the half-dark, "I've *gotta* shove off."

Lonnie takes her hand. "We were just talkin' about you, Sheila. You and bowling." He laughs and nudges me with his elbow.

I get it, Lonnie. This is her, the gal with the bowling alley brain. And I look her up and down. She's ordinary enough, dressed like she's come straight from some office, except for her shoes which give off a greenish, sparkly glow. Sheila Green Shoes, I think.

I slide four ones under the edge of my glass, but Lonnie grabs my arm again, never taking his eyes off the woman.

"One more," Lonnie says. "Hey, one more won't hurt."

"Why not?" Sheila asks, leaning around Lonnie to see my face, her eyes holding mine for a long moment.

I ease back down on the stool. "Okay, one more," I say. "Yeah, why not? But a beer this time." I look back at Sheila, her face pale in the glow from the bar, and she drops her eyes, then orders a margarita, no salt, and turns, staring at the jukebox across the room.

Sheila says something to Lonnie and they both laugh. He puts an arm around her shoulder, then leans back, digging into his pocket, and hands her some change. As she gets up she touches his leg, just brushes it with her slender fingers, and moves across the room, almost glides in those sparkly heels. She passes a table of men, ties loosened at their necks, white sleeves turned twice, then steps around the green of a pool table, a few balls scattered across its torn felt, some in and some out of a circle of light. When she reaches the little parquet dance floor her heels click for four or five steps and then all I can see is her silhouette as she blends into the Wurlitzer's glow.

"What'd I tell you, brother?" Lonnie asks. "Not bad, huh."

"Something else, Lonnie, something else." I squeeze his shoulder and move past him, following the bar to the back. I pass a pay phone and stop at the cigarette machine, staring at the choices. I could call Josie, tell her I'll be late, but decide not to, decide it's better to live with a touch of guilt now and save the fight for later. So I move back to the bar, and the twang of Willie's melancholy lyrics fills the almost empty room.

Sheila's still at the jukebox, hand on hip, her head tilted to the side, as if she's puzzling over one last selection. I pull in beside Lonnie and find a second beer glistening next to my half-empty one.

"Lonnie," I say. He turns and with a laugh starts to explain the second beer, but I cut him off, my words shooting out from some place deep inside. "Lonnie, I'm leavin' Josie."

He doesn't say anything for a minute, and I watch his grin fade into a frown. Then he says, "Uh-uh. You're puttin' me on."

I don't say anything then, just shrug and look down at my beer.

"Doesn't shock the hell out of me, Jackie," he finally says. "When?"

"I'm just waiting for a good day to leave," I say, and then tell him what I'd already figured out, about Danny's birthday coming up.

The TV comes on loud then with the game and Sheila turns to the bartender, both hands on her hips, then starts toward him. He goes over and turns it down all the way, but one of the men at the table groans, so the bartender turns it back up to a loud whisper and Sheila comes back. She takes her tailored jacket off before she sits down and I see her breasts strain, pressed tight against her blouse as she pulls her arms back. I glance at Lonnie and his eyes haven't missed a thing.

"Damn," she says. "Do they have to play on Friday night?"

"Playoffs, darlin', playoffs," Lonnie says, watching the big screen. "Doesn't happen every year, you know. Not for the Astros, anyway."

"Have you eaten?" she asks, looking at Lonnie, then over at me where her eyes linger a moment. "I'm starved. Let's go somewhere. Somewhere with food and a jukebox and no TV. How about the Tip Top?"

Lonnie grumbles and shakes his head, eyes never leaving the tube. "Go ahead, darlin'," he says. "But you can count us out."

I picture Josie, picking over some pepper beef or something, watching the clock, watching the TV. The kitchen still filled with smoke and the drone of the vent fan. Go home to that and gummy rice and sticky talk? Do I really want to know what happened at Security Bank today? At Porter Junior High?

"Lonnie," I say, "a little food wouldn't hurt. What do you think? The Tip Top's not bad."

"Hey," he says, grabbing at my sleeve. "I thought you had to get home."

He looks at me and raises his eyebrows; his forehead wrinkles. "But then I guess maybe not." Then he says, "Don't go, Jackie. Stay here. Be a hell of a game, and we can talk."

Then he turns to Sheila and reaches for her arm, but she backs away just a little. "Hey," he says. "Where you going? You're not leavin' me, are you?"

Sheila gets up and starts putting on her jacket. This time Lonnie doesn't watch, but I do. Then I see her sparkly shoes dance around Lonnie's stool toward me.

Sheila puts her hand on my arm, gives it a little squeeze. "You going or not?" she demands. Lonnie appears to have drifted away somewhere, his eyes glazed over by the light of the screen.

"Hey, what do you say?" I ask, nudging Lonnie in the side. He keeps staring straight at the TV and only shakes his head. "You don't mind, do you?" But Sheila grabs my arm and says, "Let's go."

"Meet us later," I say, but Lonnie doesn't give me a look. Shit on him, I think. It's my life and nobody, not a soon-to-be ex-wife, not a pissy-acting little brother, can tell me what to do. Hell, he's almost forty, but you'd think he's seventeen, the way he acts. Sheila leads me to the door and we slide out into the night, headed for the Tip Top.

Inside we find a corner booth and for a minute we sit, watching a fat couple jiggle around the little dance floor.

Hardly anyone's here, as if Friday nights belong to the new places with Irish names out east of town.

"You're in real estate," Sheila says. "Lonnie told me something about that."

"More or less," I say, not knowing if managing a few run-down duplexes for some jerks out of California makes me "in real estate." But if not that, then what? There isn't much else.

"Lonnie's younger?" she asks.

"Yeah, he's younger," I say and shrug. "Little brother." She sips a fresh margarita. I can see all the way to the bottom of her slow green eyes.

"You're married," she says. "He told me that, too, I think."

"More or less," I say again, but this time I laugh and she does, too.

"I know how that is," she says, giving me a sympathetic look. "Believe me, I know." And I believe her.

The waitress comes over but doesn't say a word, just stands there until we make up our minds.

Then Sheila starts telling me about her job, how she works for the state and what she does, which pretty well goes right on by me. But her talking's not the nervous kind you might expect, going on about everything just to fill up the empty space. No, she's nice and relaxed. While she talks she puts her hand on my arm and then takes it quickly back, then in a minute there it is again, this time for a little longer. I act like I don't notice.

Then she motions to the jukebox and says, "Come on, let's check it out."

We dance to a couple of songs and I can see my dinner cooling on the table, but I don't really give a damn. She's smooth and light, and what's best, she holds me when we dance as if I matter to her. And Josie and Danny and Lonnie all drift away from me and for the first time in maybe forever, *I* am light and hold a woman as if *she* matters.

Then an old Beatles song, "Hey Jude," pours out around us and she spins away and starts to sway, her eyes rolled back, her lips moving but not in sync with the words. I lean close trying to make out what she's saying, but all I can pick up is some kind of chant moving at about half speed. Oh, shit, I think, here we go, it's just like Lonnie said. The music's easy to follow, even for me, and I sway this way and that, but after a while wonder if the damn song will ever end. Finally the Beatles run down, and I stop, breathing kind of hard, but she's still moving, arms reaching for the ceiling, spinning her own slow circle. I wait there feeling like a fool, not knowing whether to get the hell off the dance floor or what. One thing I can say for Josie, she never made me feel like a fool. But in a minute Sheila snaps back in gear with a smile and a graceful lift of her head, like she's some fairy princess.

"You okay?" I ask. But she grabs my hand with a laugh and dances me back to our table.

We sit close together and eat. She just picks at her salad, and pretty soon I push my plate back and drink another beer. Her hand moves up and down my thigh under the table, and I touch her silver earring and then her ear and then her lips, as if my finger is a feather.

Then she takes my hand and places it palm up on the table, spreading it flat with both her thumbs.

"See this," she says, jabbing at the fat part of my palm. "This is the Mount of Luna." Then she traces a line from there all the way up to the base of my little finger. "And here, this is the area of Mercury."

"From the moon to Mercury," I say.

"You know this?" she asks, and I shake my head and think, hell no, I don't know this stuff. She think I'm some kind of weirdo? And I catch myself wishing I could tell Josie about my area of Mercury. Yeah, Josie might like that.

"This is good," she says, studying my hand, and I lean closer, our heads almost touching. "See the shape, like a crescent. It's turned in, see, this way." And she traces the curve over and over again with a fingernail that's the color of fresh-cut lime.

"If this curved out, you couldn't trust your intuition," she says. "But you don't have to worry. You only need to follow your heart." Then she folds my fingers up, one at a time, and holds my fist tight in both her hands.

I sense that things are moving right along, but feel a little uneasy, like Sheila's calling the shots, not just following along like Josie always does. Maybe I should go back. Lonnie'll still be there. I can catch the last couple of innings, see that all my ducks are lined up before I make a move.

But then I look up and here comes Lonnie moving towards the table, and I think, oh shit, and edge away from Sheila just a little, start to pull my hand away from hers, but she hangs on. He stops a few steps away, steadying himself on the next booth.

"Lonnie. Come on. I'll buy you a beer," I say, and point to a chair that he can pull up next to me. But he just stands there, swaying a little, a look on his face I can't quite place.

"I called her, Jackie," he says. His voice is slurred, but I hear the words clear enough and don't say a thing, just feel my heart freeze up. "God, Jackie, I'm sorry. I don't know what got into me."

"What'd you say?" I ask, not needing to ask who he had called.

"It seemed right at the time," he says. "You know, that maybe it would make things easier for you."

"You son of a bitch," I say. "You told her where I am?"

"Yeah, and who you're with. And what you told me, about leaving and all." Lonnie starts to cry, but the tears aren't from being sad. He's not sad at all.

I start to reach out a hand, but think better of it, not knowing just what it is I feel or what I might do. "What'd she say?" I ask.

"Josie said to tell you not to worry about it," he says.

"Not to worry about it. You're sure?"

"Yeah," Lonnie says, wiping one eye with a fist and fighting back his tears, almost grinning in defiance. "She says you don't have to wait anymore, not for her, not for Danny's birthday. And not to wait either for a good day to leave."

"Oh, shit," Sheila says. "She's not coming down here, is she?" And she starts to slide away.

Lonnie doesn't answer, and I put my hand on Sheila's leg and hold it tight, but I feel her skirt slipping through my fingers and then she's gone.

We're quiet a couple of minutes before either of us speaks. Then Lonnie says, "I told you Sheila's nuts. You'd have been sorry."

We sit there awhile. Lonnie orders coffee; I pull catfish off the bone with my fork.

"The game over?" I ask, knowing that it must be.

He nods.

"Astros win?"

"No," he says.

"That figures," I say. "Well, I've got to shove off."

"Where to?" Lonnie asks.

I just shrug.

"You can stay with me, Jackie," he says. "You know you can stay with me." He puts his hand on my arm.

"Yeah, and you can go to hell, Lonnie," I say, jerking my arm away. "Just go to hell."

But I sit there and stare out past him at nothing at all, and neither of us makes a move to leave.

Ducks

WHILE Darrel drives, Maureen practices, sighting with the hood ornament of the pickup, lining up the V between the ram's horns with the cars they meet. She aims, waiting for the right moment, and then, with her cheeks puffed just a little, makes a small "poof" sound, soft so Darrel won't hear. She's a great shot, a natural. Darrel always says it's her hand/eye coordination. Then he tells her she should have played basketball and laughs. Easy for him to say, she thinks, like there's a talent to being tall.

The road narrows down to two lanes and the pickup slows, making it easy. Three cows waiting in a grazed-out field. Poof, poof, poof. A tractor pulling a trailer of corn. Poof, poof. The driver, too, poof, an old man with a faded high school letter jacket pulled tight around him. Maureen used to shy away from drivers, and still won't line up women, but for men it's open season. She looks back. The tractor chugs along the shoulder, tilted to one side, the old man getting smaller, hunkering down in the wind.

"Ducks'll be sailing in ninety miles a hour," Darrel tells her, leaning forward in the seat. He tilts his head to one side, checking the weather below the green of the windshield tint. The sky is smooth as cream gravy, but darker, a fresh norther hurrying the clouds south. "Girlfriend, if it don't rain," Darrel says, "whoo-ee, we'll slaughter 'em. Ducks'll be thicker'n July mosquitoes."

Maureen lines up the swirl of a cloud with a corner of the window visor. Poof.

Maureen hated guns until she shot one. And even now, after years of hunting, the noise still bothers her, the way the little twenty-gauge roars and leaves her with a tingle of numbness, a mosquito hum that sticks in her jawbone for hours afterwards. But the kick against her shoulder makes it all worthwhile, the way it rocks her back, vibrates down, shakes her insides like a dollar's worth of Magic Fingers, somewhere deep. It started out as fear but long ago had gone beyond that. More than fear, although guns still scare her, and more than the power that she feels cradling the gun in the loop of her arm. Too intense for that kind of power. Darrel teases her about it, tells her, Girlfriend, you finally found your G spot.

Not quite that. But something. Maybe feeling equal. Maybe not being just a girl, although at thirty-seven that shouldn't still be a problem. Oh, well, she sighs.

Some things Maureen doesn't like about duck hunting: first, the drive. Cottonwood is four boring hours north out of Houston over the same black patched roads, through the same brittle towns. Darrel doesn't believe in interstates, says they ruined the little towns and he'd rather spend his dollars for gas and whatever going the back way.

Maureen buys that. She works mornings at a Bailey's Green Thumb. She likes it even if after taxes her take-home just covers Darrel's child support and maybe an on-sale Dillard's blouse. Maureen hates those monthly checks to Robot. Robot is what Maureen calls Roberta who was Darrel's dizzy wife when they met. Maureen can't stand sending Robot *her* money.

But she's crazy about the work. The watering and deadheading and feeding, checking for aphids and spider mites and black spot. You wouldn't know it, walking into a nursery, all green and blossomy, that every morning there's a dead pile and a terminal row out back. The terminals hardly ever pull through. Maureen knows this but tries anyway. It's tricky. Too much of anything—water, fertilizer, sun, shade, or too little of the same. Terminals one day, dead pile the next.

That's all that Maureen can see, either side of Highway 59, terminals here, dead piles there. Small businesses and small towns may be, as Darrel says, the heart of America, but they'll grind you down or bore you to death between heartbeats.

So the drive is one thing. Another is the ducks dying. Not the killing of them, which anyone will admit is sport enough and damned hard, even for a person with remarkably abundant hand/eye coordination like Maureen. And not the ducks being dead, which is what happens to ducks anyway sooner or later, and they're always plucked and the soft underbelly feathers saved for pillows and plush, squishy cushions that make the softest what otherwise would be unaffordable Christmas gifts. The ducks are not wasted. This is not count-to-see-how-many or mount-them-on-the-wall kind of hunting. This is in-the-blood-take-me-back-forever hunting. A let-us-kill-them-so-that-we-may-live, deep-in-your-bones kind of ritual. The kind you may not know about, but it's in your bones, too, and not touched anymore in the Safeway mentality you may be used to of here's $4.50 for your frozen duck with the separately packaged liver, gizzard, and heart. Shooting and plucking and gutting just a

way to get to the splitting and grilling or stuffing and baking. A way to get to the picking and sucking of meat, dark
and rich, from their bony little body cages with no remorse
whatsoever.

So it's not the killing, and not the being dead, that bothers Maureen. It's the dying. The way a duck, with a cracked
and crippled wing, weighted with a half-load scattershot of
number four pellets, will paddle it seems like forever in a
tiny one-winged circle, and you on the shore knowing another blast would put it away, but knowing, also, that one
more blast of shot will shred and tear and waste both feathers and meat, so you try not to watch the circle as it slows,
watching instead the light sinking over the tree-shadowed
lake, hoping that the circling will be stopped, that the duck
will die and the wind won't, at least not before the little lake
waves ride its limp body within long-limb range of the
shore. And hoping that Darrel won't notice you haven't
shot again since winging that one and that you can't slide
another three plastic-coated smooth-snapping shells into
the breech. Not yet. The little twenty-gauge pump empty
and hot and blue and always obedient. It seems to get worse
every year, waiting for the wounded ducks to die.

Maureen marks each year by that peculiar season. Eleven
duck seasons, eleven years of marriage, eleven years older. A
slow process, life is.

So the drive is boring and the ducks are living, then
they're dying, then they're dead.

Maureen is used to this, she accepts, she adjusts, she
knows she doesn't have to go along. Shouldn't have to prove
herself, not again. Good hand/eye won't go away, not all at
once.

Grady is the problem. And Ruby, too. But mostly Grady.
In one way Maureen hopes that Grady won't go out hunting
with them, that he'll sit around on his mama's saggy sofa all
afternoon and root for the Aggies. But he'll go. Maureen
knows, and she wants him to for Darrel. Grady and Darrel

might as well be brothers, Ruby raising them both, taking in
Darrel when he was still little. Darrel's mama crippled with
MS. His daddy stacked five tens on the kitchen table and
disappeared. Not even a goodbye note.

From the very first Darrel was right up front, letting her
know it was a package deal. You get me, he told Maureen,
you get Ruby and Grady. Ruby she could take, crankiness
and all she had a big heart. But Grady? It seems like once a
year she could stand him, especially on Thanksgiving, and
more especially since the hunt means so much to Darrel.

Grady didn't mind when Maureen first came along. He
seemed to like it she could handle a gun, had a sure eye,
would help clean the ducks. Maureen didn't know what had
changed, maybe just that the new had worn off and Grady
wanted things the way they were before. His jokes started
getting dirtier, he held his once-a-year hug a little longer,
uncomfortably longer, and tighter. Whatever it was, Maureen had felt the tension between the two of them build
every year. At first she ignored Grady, then finally tried to
talk it out with Darrel, but that only puzzled and hurt him.
Now Maureen obsessed about Grady, dreaded the trip up,
stretching out the unpleasantness over several days rather
than living with it for an afternoon. It disgusted Maureen
that a man in his forties would live with his mother,
wouldn't have a place of his own. But Ruby was the kind of
mama that didn't seem to mind.

Three years back it was awful. It began to sleet before
noon and kept on all day, turning the streets slick with ice,
trapping Maureen there in the house. All day and into the
night with Darrel and Grady and Ruby, the men easing back
and forth, slipping around like they were still boys, but now
out to the garage, sitting up on the hood of Ruby's ancient
Plymouth. They badly damaged a quart of Old Fitz, coming
back through the kitchen, grazing on some leftover dressing
or a pickled onion to kill the smell. Way past mellow by the
third quarter. All the time Maureen stuck dark in the front

room with pruny Ruby, becoming world expert number one on Church of the Nazarene and why Catholics aren't really genuine Christians. You want ducks, Girlfriend, Darrel told her, that's the price you pay. Sand Lake has the ducks, Ruby's farm has Sand Lake, Grady has Ruby for a mama. You're lucky, just going along for a free ride. Hummph, Maureen said to herself.

Thanksgiving morning. Not much traffic. Maureen lines up fence posts. Poof, poof, poof. Then every third yellow stripe on the road. Poof, da, da, poof, da da, poof. Maureen, you're getting compulsive about this, she thinks, but everywhere she looks something lines up. Poof.

"Did you ever wonder," she says to Darrel, "what if that night we met you had gone with Robot to the Nightmare Cafe instead of to the Chili Parlor and found me?"

Darrel kind of grunts and keeps looking straight ahead, his eyebrows bushing up almost to the brim of his cap.

"What If" is Maureen's favorite traveling game. "What if this? What if I had a mastectomy? Would you still love me? Would you wish you still had Robot?"

"Don't even think things like that, Girlfriend," Darrel says. He reaches over and squeezes Maureen's arm. He's frowning real hard. Too hard? Maureen wonders. She thinks he will feel her breast, but he doesn't. She's glad, but also kind of disappointed. She has nice breasts, she likes them. Big enough to be full and need good support, but not so big as to be show-offy. She knows Darrel loves her breasts, but she sometimes worries about the rest of her. Not her looks— she has been called striking, but she's a little short, she knows, and her calves have started thickening, losing the nice curve they once had. So what, she thinks. That's not to be worried over. She wears jeans a lot. Maureen worries about other things, what's inside both of them that she can't see.

"What if you had only three months to live, sweetheart. What would you do?" she asks. "Really, now, what would you do?"

Darrel slows the truck and puts on his turn blinker. Maureen sees the Hasty Tasty off to the left. "Well, Girlfriend, let's see," he says. "First thing I'd do is tackle a foot-long chili dog. How about you?"

They pull to a stop on the gravel lot and Darrel says, "How about it?" Maureen says, "Chocolate malt," and slides down in the seat. She watches Darrel at the to-go window. He stretches, then bends over, peering into a newspaper box. She lines him up with the ram on the hood, aiming right at the heart of his camouflage vest. Poof.

It's drizzling. Maureen waits in the truck, blowing from down deep on the side window, huuh, huuh. Trying to fit all the fogged-up breath rings together. Darrel's helping Grady with his guns, his cooler, sliding everything around under the camper top. Darrel grunts, working in a crouch. Maureen feels the truck rock from side to side when he moves. Then Grady shouts something back at the house and stomps away, a mixed set of duck decoys slung over his shoulder. She hears Grady say no problem, no problem. Darrel appears at her window. She rolls it halfway down and he pushes her jacket through.

"Want to say hi to Ruby before we go?"

"Do I need a blessing before I hunt?"

"I guess not," Darrel says.

"Then no. Hell no."

"She's not bad to you, Girlfriend." Darrel opens the door and turns his head sideways. He has a do-it-for-me-please-I-love-you look on his face that she knows will change to a do-it-for-me-or-I'll-be-pissy-the-rest-of-the-day look if she doesn't.

"Okay," Maureen says, and steps down. Darrel hustles back to the house, stomping his feet on a newspaper at the side door.

She nods at Grady.

He's carrying a leather gun case by the handle and a vest

full of brass-top shells. He pushes his cap back on his head. "How you doing, hot shot. Ready for a little action?"

"Ready for the ducks," Maureen says.

"I'll bet you are," Grady says. "Always ready."

Ruby's in the kitchen, getting coffee, talking, telling about Roy Dale, her brother, who had triple bypass. "A cigarette," she says. "Still under the oxygen tent and asking for a cigarette. Might as well pull the plug on him. But he always was like that, you know."

"It's going to fall down around her," Maureen whispers. She and Darrel are sitting in the dining room around a square oak table that's covered with a tattered crochet-fringed white-at-one-time tablecloth. Maureen's eyeing the ceiling where wallpaper hangs in giant brown swirls from rotted canvas.

"It's always been that way," Darrel says and shrugs.

"Always? Always?"

Darrel puts one finger to his lips.

"God," Maureen says. She folds her arms tight, hugging herself, and pushes back against the knobbly rungs of her chair.

Ruby comes back in the room. She's carrying a flowery TV tray filled with cups and napkins. "And then when Roy Dale finally gets home, what does Doris do but sit right there next to him, reading trashy magazines and blowing smoke in his face. You take cream, Maureen?" Ruby says Moreen, with a long *o*. "Clogs your arteries and all, you know."

"Cream and sugar," Maureen says. Black, she thinks. For eleven years I've been coming here, drinking my coffee black. If the old biddy can't remember. Darrel narrows his eyes at her. Oh, well.

"Smell that, Darrel?" Ruby asks. She lifts her head and turns toward the kitchen, looking over the tops of her glasses. Crossed bobby pins hold four little gray curls tight against her splotchy forehead. "Your favorite, Darrel. But you know. Moreen," she says. She turns to Maureen. "What is it, Moreen? You'll never guess."

"Sweet potato casserole with marshmallows," Maureen says, knowing she's being a smartass, that she's not trying. "And turkey and cornbread dressing and—mince pie?"

"No, no, no. Not mince pie. You know I never could stand mince pie. Darrel, you know. Tell Moreen what it is."

"Pecan pie," Maureen says quickly, before Darrel can answer, and Ruby's face falls. God, am I so competitive? Maureen thinks. Do I always have to win? No, not always. Only here.

"Good eye, good nose." It's Grady, just inside the door, watching for how long Maureen doesn't know. "No telling what else that girl can do."

"Well, I know she's talented," Ruby says. "Only talented girls ever fell for Darrel."

Grady coughs and grins. He's standing there, leaning against the door frame. He stares at Maureen.

"Hey, we better get going," Darrel says, looking at his watch. "Dinner at dark-thirty, Ruby?" he asks. But Ruby's already in the kitchen.

While Darrel drives he watches ahead just enough to keep the pickup in the road. He looks around, taking in Cottonwood as they maneuver around the square and head out east of town. Back in Cottonwood Darrel gets a puzzled look on his face. Maureen used to worry about it, that way of looking, wondered if Darrel was trying to spot old girlfriends. Now she thinks Cottonwood disorients him, he's puzzled the way the years have moved on by and how he's ended up.

Maureen stares straight ahead, refusing to look at Grady. Up close, his face is all craters, whorls and peaks, a tiny, ruddy moonscape. He has yellow teeth that show when he grins, and he grins a lot, too much for Maureen. He keeps looking around Maureen at Darrel, working his shoulder back and forth against hers.

Grady talks, all the while popping his neck to one side. It's bothered him for years, or so he says. Maureen guesses a stillson wrench from the top of a derrick could do some damage. Grady showed her the hard hat he wore. Buckled right down the middle. Maureen watches the hairs on the back of Grady's hand, the way he punches the padded dash with one stubby finger as he talks. She tunes in, she tunes out.

"So there I am," Grady's saying, "in this frigging little johnboat, a three-and-a-half Johnson that keeps choking down in the damned duckweed, out in the frigging middle of Caddo Lake. I'm working cypress stumps with a Hula Popper and all of sudden, just like that, the damned lake turns to a mirror. Still, you know, like you've never seen still. Everything stopped. And there coming out of the south this thunderhead, black as a hairy whale, already sitting right on top of me."

"No shit," Darrel says, and Grady shakes his head. "Man," Grady says, and pulls a half pint of whiskey out of his jacket, "I swore and be damned if I'd ever touch liquor, dance with wild women, or throw craps again, if only the Lord would get me through that one."

"Didn't last long," Maureen says.

"Two out of three's okay," Grady says, and takes a big swig from the bottle and slaps the dash hard. "Uh-uh," he says, "never again all three, not at once that is," and he passes the bottle to Darrel.

"You're driving, sweetheart," Maureen says.

For a minute Darrel just stares straight ahead, on hesitate, just like the windshield wipers. He concentrates, holding the bottle on one knee. Maureen sees nothing but gray out there, can't see even a line where the highway meets the sky. She puts her hand on Darrel's leg and squeezes.

Darrel holds the bottle out and nods at Grady. He says,

"Here's to ducks, fat and low and slow." Then he tilts the bottle way back and takes a big swig.

Grady lets out a big "Yahoo."

Maureen says, "Oh, shit."

Before the lake's even in sight they pull off on a gravelly spot and park. Maureen asks why here, and Darrel tells her you never go past where you can turn around, nodding his head as if he were some wise old woodsman. Maureen hates it when Darrel gets this way, when he turns into a know-it-all, talking like his was the very last never-to-be-questioned word on everything. Maureen blames it on Grady, like his little smirk somehow beams across into Darrel's head.

Their boots suck away from black gumbo as they move, Grady off to the right already in a line of trees, loaded down with decoys. Darrel beginning to crouch as they get closer, even though he and Maureen are in the open, following a rutted cut of a road that slices through the woods, crouching as if ducks can't see him that way. At the edge of the lake he straightens up and looks around. Then he breaks open his double-barrel. "Too early for ducks," Maureen says.

Darrel looks out over the lake. "You never can tell," he says.

They retreat a dozen or so steps from the water's edge. The woods here are dense, ropy with grapevines as thick as a man's arm. Darrel kicks a pile of wet leaves out from under a bare red oak and covers it with his slicker. He and Maureen ease themselves down, sitting back to back; Grady straddles a stump off to one side. He passes the bottle to Darrel, who reaches it around to Maureen. She wiggles her head from side to side. "Why not?" she says, and takes a half sip. She holds it in her mouth a minute, then lets the heat ease down her throat, hoping it'll reach her toes. The drizzle has stopped. She pulls on the barrel of her twenty-gauge with her gloved hand like you'd milk a cow, leaving it streaky dry. She pulls the gun tight against her shoulder and aims at nothing, sweeping the barrel to the left and then back to the right, making the little poof sound each time. She looks around then and sees Grady watching her, stretching his neck one way then the other.

"Pretty easy without ducks," Grady says with a little laugh. Darrel lets out a trace of a laugh, too, and when it fades all you can hear is some kind of bird scratching at the leaves.

In a while they split up. Maureen moves to the edge of the lake, where she can see the gravel bottom clear as an aquarium. Little schools of minnows tease the surface. She crouches under a clump of bare willows, then swings her gun up and around. Uh-uh. The arching limbs crisscross her line of fire. She moves off to her left and finds a clump of cattails and eases down in them, making a nest of sorts. She's glad it's winter and the water moccasins are deep in the mud or wherever. She settles in, tries to get comfortable, so she won't have to move. Darrel told her that being in sight's not important. Being dead-still is. As if she'd never hunted before. Just because Darrel works night security in a Baytown refinery he sees himself as some kind of super-sleuth.

Maureen spots Darrel, moving around the perimeter of the lake. He looks tiny against the woods. She looks for Grady to appear across the narrow part of the lake. That was the plan. Darrel at the far end, near where the west point of the lake once fed into the river, and Grady straight across, a hundred yards or so from Maureen. Darrel called it his triangle strategy, a way to hem in the ducks.

Maureen hears a low whistle behind her. Not one of those downtown Houston hard-hat whistles, but a soft, low, three-in-a-row dovelike whistle.

"Mo-reen. Mo-reen." Grady steps out from behind an oak tree, cradling his shotgun in the crook of his arm. He holds out the pint bottle with one hand and wipes the top with the other. It's nearly empty.

"What," she says, and stands up. Her voice echoes quiet and smooth among the trees, but her insides feel light, uneasy.

"Want a swig?" he says. "Come here." He motions for her to come, holding out the bottle like she was a bird he could tempt closer with a slice of bread. He looks up to the end of the lake where Darrel is and takes a step or two toward her.

With her finger and thumb Maureen flips the safety of the gun off and on, off and on. Without looking she sees it. Red and black, red and black.

"You're drunk, Grady," she says.

"Uh-uh, Hot Shot," he says. "Just close to feeling good. I like feeling good. Don't you?"

"Get lost, Grady," Maureen says. "That's your side of the lake." She jerks her thumb back over her shoulder at the water.

"I tell you what," he says. "Let's have a little contest. See who can drop the most ducks. I win and you give me whatever I want. You win—well, you can name it."

"Uh-uh, Grady. There's nothing of yours I want. Just take a hike."

"A friendly little contest," he says. "That's what you like, isn't it? Competition? Might as well not shoot if nothing's on the line." He slips the bottle back in his jacket pocket then and starts to go. "You keep count. I trust you." He laughs then and disappears back into the woods.

Maureen nests back down in the cattails. She watches Darrel setting out a string of decoys, maneuvering a little rowboat, pushing the decoys around with a long pole. Then he's swallowed up by the gray of some brush.

Maureen feels flat; the little buzz from the bourbon is gone and has left her empty. She hopes the ducks stayed in Canada this year. Grady appears across the lake and strings out the other decoys in a half ring. They wait.

Four little wood ducks come in low behind Darrel, but he

sees them too late and they veer off and up, out of range, wings whistling. Jesus, they're fast, Maureen thinks.

For some reason they circle back and Darrel gets off two quick shots. One duck drops in the trees. Darrel stands up to spot it and crouches back down.

Then it really starts. A bunch of mallards, big, flashes of color, their wings fill the air. Maureen rises. Shoots. Reloads. Then another group of eight or nine. What are they? Greenheads, maybe teals. Grady bags one, then misses with two quick blasts. She hears his shot splatter leaves as it drops like sleet just behind her in the woods. From that distance getting peppered with shot is harmless, more discourteous than dangerous. Maureen mutters "bastard" under her breath.

A half hour before dusk the ducks come in waves. Maureen keeps count despite herself. Darrel still has only the one wood duck, but has scared several flights down the lake. She and Grady have three ducks apiece. Then suddenly the ducks stop coming and the lake is still. A half moon is now visible, pale against the gray sky. Maureen watches it, the way a wisp of clouds slides across its face. She feels a vague uneasiness, a sadness she can't quite place.

Right at dark a pair of ducks whistles down the middle of the lake. A little far, Maureen knows, but figures if she doesn't try, then Grady will. It's automatic, the smooth swing of her gun, the lead calculated unconsciously, eyeing height and distance and speed. Blam, blam. One duck tumbles in a spiral, still flapping, losing control. A splash and then quickly, like a cork, it bobs upright. Then twice, and then a third time tries to splash itself back up into the darkening sky, but can't. It swims up-lake a short way, then stops, as if to rest. Maureen knows what to do. Stiffly she stands and reloads, then makes her way up the edge of the water, getting closer, dreading to take that final shot.

The duck is paddling in circles now, moving away, struggling in a slow spiral toward the other bank. She feels sick inside watching it. Come on, she tells herself and pulls the gun tight against her shoulder. It's not the killing, it's the dying, she says. Do it, do it, do it.

"I'll do it, Hot Shot." Grady has moved as she moved, and now is directly across from her, actually closer than Maureen to the wounded duck. His gun is raised. Their voices carry easily across the water.

"That's my duck, Grady."

"Wingin' don't count, Hot Shot."

The duck keeps paddling, circling farther up-lake, now out of range. Maureen scrambles along the edge. She splashes through a little draw, hugging the gun to her chest, watching Grady move on the other shore.

She stops again. Her breath pushes out, puffs of white in the half-dark. The duck is now just a black spot on the shimmer of the lake. It's my duck, she thinks. I don't have to kill it if I don't want to. Come morning I could trap it, care for it, let it heal. "Grady," she says, her voice high, pleading across the lake where Grady is no more than a shadow with a gun. She hears Darrel, from the end of the lake, "Girlfriend!"

Then the first blast rocks across the water. Followed by a second, then a third. Maureen hears Grady give a whoop, then laugh. "One up on you, Hot Shot. Four to three. Grady wins." He laughs again, a deep throaty laugh, one that echoes through the trees.

Maureen looks at the moon, tries to see the dark half, can make out an outline of sorts. She pumps the gun. One, two, three shells thud at her feet. It's just a game, she thinks, just a game for big little boys. But not for me. No more.

Then she takes the gun by its barrel, grips it as close to the end as she can with both hands and feels a strength she's never had. She holds the gun out from her body, arms extended, and starts to circle. The weight of the gun pulls her as she spins. She leans back, turning on her heels, slowly at first, then whirling, faster and faster, finally releasing the gun with a gasp, letting it go, letting everything go, hearing the gun spin, ka-whoosh, ka-whoosh, ka-whoosh out over the lake and into the night.

Flying

B EN RAY has a girlfriend. Aunt Marlene had spotted him with a strange woman when he stopped at the Circle K for his weekly carton of Camels. She first got suspicious when he picked up a couple of packs of Winstons, too. Then she noticed that Ben Ray had wheeled his pickup around to the side of the store and out of sight where he left it running, instead of pulling right big up front like always before. That's when Aunt Marlene knew for sure that something out of the ordinary was cooking.

So when Ben Ray hurried out the door without even a quick free peek inside a *Playboy* or his usual smartass comment, Aunt Marlene just followed him right outside into that lit-up night like she was going to check a gas pump, but turned and stared around the corner of the store as Ben Ray eased off down the side street.

"Your daddy was all nervous like a teenager on a first date," she later told Sara. And the woman, "made up like a Dallas lady for sure, with a big bunch of cotton candy hair."

After that Sara noticed that her daddy acted different. Ben Ray no longer frowned or gave her a hard time when she asked to sleep over at her cousin Deanie's on Friday nights. He even brought pizza home for supper sometimes in the middle of the week. Sara figured that if a girlfriend made Ben Ray act that way, then a girlfriend was all right with her.

On that next Saturday morning Ginger, Sara's big sister, called Sara at Deanie's. "Why don't you and Deanie come out to Grandma's? You can help me."

"Do what?" Sara asked. "Will you come and pick us up?"

"Just come on out," Ginger said. "You can ride your bikes. You don't want to get fat like Ben Ray, do you?"

Sara knew that ever since Ben Ray had kicked Ginger out of the house for showing back up in town with Bronson, her baby, and no husband even hinted at, she poked at their daddy every chance she got. And Sara guessed that Ben Ray was a little overweight, maybe, but that didn't bother her. What did bother her was the thought, for the first time ever, that she might grow up and look like Ben Ray. Everybody had always said that Ginger was just like Pearl, their mama, skinny and all. But until then Sara had never thought about being like anyone but herself. She was only twelve, and she knew she would change, but exactly how she had never even given a thought. Sara wasn't fat, but she wasn't skinny, either, not like Ginger or even Deanie. She was a bit thick, was all, her arms and her legs stocky and fleshy, and she tried to imagine Ben Ray as a twelve-year-old boy who maybe had been built the same way. But all that would come to her mind was silly—a vision of Ben Ray's big bushy head on the body of a stocky little boy, so she gave up.

Sara and Deanie bicycled out to the edge of town and turned down the Farm-to-Market road that led out to Grandma Strange's. At first Sara pedaled furiously, leaving

Deanie complaining and far behind. She stood up as she rode, pumping hard to stretch her legs until she could almost feel them getting longer and slimmer.

Sara leaned her bike against the side of Grandma Strange's house and waited for Deanie, then they went inside. The kitchen dinette was covered with scattered piles of corn kernels next to pans of red and blue and turquoise dye. Newspapers spread out in one corner of the floor were covered with piles of the colored kernels.

"See this?" Ginger asked, holding up several strands of strung blue corn. "This is my ticket out of here."

"What is it?" Sara asked.

"Come on, Sara. Don't you know anything? Deanie, you know, don't you?"

Deanie just stared at all the corn.

"These are Indian corn necklaces," Ginger explained as she held one up around her neck. "Or at least they will be when I get the fasteners on. They sell like crazy in New Mexico. A dollar apiece for me. Can you believe it. They don't cost hardly a dime to make."

Deanie rolled her eyes at the ceiling, but Ginger kept on like she was trying to convert the girls or something. Below all the words Sara could hear the strain in Ginger's voice, just a little, like she was really down deep saying believe me, believe me, and for the first time maybe ever Sara felt a twinge of embarrassment for her older sister.

Ginger handed Sara and Deanie big needles and some colored thread. "Here," she said. "If you two are gonna hang around then you might as well help out. You both do red. I'm short of red ones. Count carefully now. A hundred kernels to a strand."

Deanie snorted. "Real Indians use real Indian corn," she said. "Not deer corn with a bunch of Rit on it."

"Who cares?" Ginger asked. "The tourists won't know the difference anyway."

"I would," Deanie said, and Ginger glared at her.

"You're not as smart as you think," Ginger said, and Deanie stuck out her tongue when her cousin turned away.

It wasn't easy. The kernels were hard and some split when Sara forced the needle through. But Ginger gave her little tips, things she had learned, like sticking the needle first in a bar of soap, and pretty soon Sara caught on. Sara asked Ginger what she knew about Ben Ray's girlfriend, but Ginger didn't answer, concentrating hard on mixing a new batch of dye. "It can't be just any old color, you know. If you'd been there, actually lived in New Mexico as long as I have, you'd know that."

Deanie said the dye was too yucky and started teasing Bronson, who up until then had been content in his playpen.

Ginger leaned against the kitchen counter and nibbled at a biscuit from a pan on the stove. Grandma Strange mixed up a batch of biscuits every morning, just like she had when Grandpa Strange had been alive. Buttermilk biscuits, big as Ben Ray's fist. By noon only a couple would be gone and Grandma Strange tossed the leftovers to the chickens.

"Okay, Sara," she said. "You want to know about Ben Ray's girlfriend, do you?" Her voice got tight and brittle like it always did when she talked about Ben Ray. She eased herself up on the counter and crossed her legs at her ankles. Her tummy bulged softly over her jeans.

Maybe Ginger won't be skinny forever after all, Sara thought.

Ginger glanced at the closed door that led to the back room where Grandma Strange was stuck in front of the TV. She lowered her voice a little and grinned. "Well, it's like Pearl says, 'Bubble hair means bubble head.' "

Deanie snortled.

"I never heard Mama say anything like that," Sara said.

"There's lots you've never heard your mama say, little sister. Just remember, I lived with Pearl for more than just a few months." Ginger whistled low and mysteriously, like she knew so much more than Sara, and moved over to one of the pans to stir the corn.

In only a few minutes Sara's fingers were sore from pushing on the needle and red from the dye.

"Will this stuff come off?" she asked, holding up her hands.

"Not real easy," Ginger said.

"Only on the tourists," Deanie said.

"You don't have to stay, Deanie," Ginger said. "If you can't help being a smart-mouth, you can just leave right now. In fact I wish you would so Sara and I can get this done."

"It's not your house," Deanie said. "You can't tell me to leave if it's not your house." Then Deanie shuffled towards the door. "But who would want to stay here, anyway?"

Deanie opened the door, then looked back at Sara. "Ben Ray said you were supposed to stay with me," she said. "He made you promise. I heard him."

Sara looked at Ginger, but she just shrugged. Then Sara looked at her fingers, all red from the Rit and sore on the ends. "Well, I guess I'd better go, too. Ben Ray might get mad if I stay."

"That's right," Ginger said, and Sara could feel the whip of her words. "Ben Ray's little girl had better mind."

Then Ginger slapped her hand hard on the counter. "Oh, just go. And come back when you're alone and not being such a baby."

"That's great," Deanie said. She banged the door shut when she left.

Sara washed her hands, getting some of the red to fade to pink. Out the window she watched Deanie fiddle with her bike, waiting. Ginger had her nose back down in one of the pots of dye, stirring some more, and didn't say a word when Sara slipped out the door.

When the girls got to Sara's house Deanie got a drink from the garden hose and sprayed Ben Ray's pickup in the process. Sara said, "I'm going to tell," but Deanie just laughed when Sara went inside. It was only a little after four, but the sky was smoothed over with a chocolate layer of clouds and the house was dark, all the venetian blinds drawn down like it was already night.

Most Saturday afternoons Ben Ray would be half asleep on the sofa, and the house filled with echoes from some football game. But the house was quiet. An empty wine bottle sat on the table along with half a sack of chips.

Deanie came in then. "Let's go for a ride," she said.

"Where to?" Sara whined. "There's nowhere to go."

"The clay pits," Deanie said. "There's always somebody there."

Then Deanie saw the wine bottle. "Does Ben Ray drink this stuff?" she asked, holding the bottle up to the light, then sniffing it. "Uhhmm. Not bad."

"You don't know," Sara said.

"I do too know," Deanie said.

Just then Ben Ray called Sara. His voice was distant and muffled like he was talking through a door.

"Pumpkin," he called. "Is that you?"

"Uh-huh," Sara called out. "Me and Deanie."

"Come here a minute, Pumpkin."

"You're in trouble, I bet," Deanie said. "Ben Ray told you to stay with me. You should have listened."

"It's my house, too," Sara said, and moved down the hall towards Ben Ray's bedroom."

The door was open a crack. She could just see Ben Ray's eyes as he talked. The room behind him was dark.

"I thought you were going to stay at Deanie's, Pumpkin."

"We got hungry," Sara said. She crossed her fingers behind her back. "And bored. There's nothing to eat and nothing to do at Deanie's."

Ben Ray turned and said "Damn" under his breath. "Just a minute, Pumpkin." He closed the door and Sara could hear him whispering, and then she picked up another voice, a woman's, one that sounded angry or impatient. Then Ben Ray opened the door again and slipped a five dollar bill through the crack.

"Get something to eat, Pumpkin, and go to Deanie's. And stay there until I call you. You understand?"

"Yessir," Sara said, although she wasn't sure she understood everything."

"I mean it now," Ben Ray said. "Go on." The door closed and the lock clicked.

Sara and Deanie took the half bag of chips and bicycled down to Side's Store. Deanie wanted to know everything that had happened, but Sara raced on ahead with her head up so that the wind washed across her face and her straight brown hair almost twisted into curls. Sara bought a frozen ice cream pie with strawberry preserves on the top and didn't care if she ever got skinny or not. Deanie bought two cigarettes for twenty cents from old man Sides and they rolled their bikes out behind the store and sat in the sun.

"Could you see Bubble Head?" Deanie asked. "She was probably naked, or maybe in some floozy nightgown."

"I heard her," Sara said. "That's all. She sounded grouchy and cranky and I hope I never have to see her."

"You get used to it," Deanie said. She blew little rings of smoke in the still air, then tried to stick her finger through them. "I have a daddy, too, you know. The same way you have Pearl. But you're lucky. I've had to go through two more daddies and lots of boyfriends that didn't stay around."

"This is different," Sara said.

"Just because Bubble Head's the first. You'll get used to it."

"You just don't understand," Sara said. She pulled her T-shirt up to lick off a blob of strawberry jam. "Ben Ray's different."

"Mama says men are all the same," Deanie said.

"Yeah, and Aunt Marlene's so smart she's probably gonna own the Sack It and Pack It pretty soon. Right?"

Deanie gave Sara a you're-not-so-smart kind of look and scraped the butt of her last cigarette on a rock. "Let's go," she said, and took off on her bike with Sara right behind.

A couple of miles out of town Deanie turned down a gravel road and after a few minutes of rough riding they came upon a long metal barn. Deanie got off her bike and looked around. The place was deserted. The back of the barn was open all the way across, and inside, cocked back on their tails, were two airplanes side by side. A grassy runway stretched out and away from the big barn, and a half-dozen brindle cows grazed their way slowly across it.

Deanie opened the door of one plane and pulled herself up and in.

"You're gonna get caught," Sara said, looking around. But they were all alone.

"Come on, Sara, don't be a nerd. We'll hear if anybody drives up. Besides, we're not hurting anything."

Sara climbed in the other side. There were clocks and dials and levers everywhere. The leather seat crunched when she settled in and everything smelled like cigarette smoke.

"Put your seat belt on," Deanie commanded. "Now close your eyes and tell me where you want to go. Anywhere in the world. Disneyland? Six Flags? Padre Island? Anywhere."

Sara giggled and closed her eyes. She thought hard, trying to envision all of those places and a whole bunch of others, but all she could see was the slice of Ben Ray's flushed face and the annoyed look in his eyes when he peeked through the almost-closed door.

"I know," Deanie said. "How about New Mexico?"

And Sara, with her eyes still closed, tried to envision the mountains and snow and skiing and the big Husky dog that Pearl had, and the way it might feel to be swaying on the back of a motorcycle, her arms wrapped tight around Pearl's waist, winding around some mountain curve.

"New Mexico," Sara said. "Yeah, that will be all right." The key was in the ignition, attached to a good-luck rabbit's foot key chain, and Deanie gave it a half turn. The lights on the dash glowed green in the dim light.

"All right!" Deanie shouted, and bounced in the seat. Then she leaned forward to check everything out.

"You better not," Sara said. "Turn it off." She grabbed her door handle. "I'll tell Aunt Marlene and Ben Ray and everybody."

"Ben Ray wouldn't even care," Deanie said. "All he can think about is Bubble Head. That's the way men are. That's what Mama says and she knows all about men."

"Ben Ray would too care," Sara said. She felt her face flush and knew it was getting splotchy the way she hated. All of a sudden Sara felt heavy and tired, and she wished she hadn't eaten the whole pie.

Deanie ignored her. She was studying the dials and gauges, pulling back on the wheel and turning it this way and that.

"You know," she said, "I think I could fly this thing. Uncle Porter's told me all about flying. He says there's nothing to it."

"He can't fly a plane," Sara said. "He's never flown one, I'll bet."

"He rode in them," Deanie said. "All the time in Vietnam. He says flying is easy."

Deanie turned the key again. This time a little farther, and the engine gave a quick bark. The plane jumped a little but didn't start. Then Deanie tried it again and the propeller caught with a roar.

"Wow!" Deanie yelled, and Sara started to yell back at her. She wanted to climb out of the plane, but she felt too heavy to move.

Sara just sank down in her seat and let everything go. She didn't want to go back to Grandma Strange's anymore, not now that Ginger and Bronson were living there, and she couldn't go back to her own house while Ben Ray and Bubble Head were still locked in the back bedroom, and at

Deanie's, Uncle Porter would be hanging around, drinking beer and acting creepy.

Sara closed her eyes and squirmed down in the leather seat as far as she could go, and felt herself sinking just as the plane began to inch forward. She kept her eyes shut tight and felt the plane pull slowly from the barn and turn. Then the wheels bumped a little as they picked up speed on the grassy runway. She heard the angry bellow of a cow as they raced along, and then the plane lifted off with a vibration that she felt all through her body.

Oh my God, she thought, but didn't dare open her eyes and look down. She felt the plane turn in a big circle as it climbed, then straighten out as it headed west and into the late afternoon sun. Even with her eyes closed she could sense the bright flashes of sunlight when they sailed between clouds.

In just a few hours they would be in New Mexico. She would call Pearl and they would roar away on the motorcycle to her cabin up in the mountains and sit before a huge fireplace and drink hot chocolate and feed special New Mexico dog biscuits to the Husky. She would write Ben Ray a long letter explaining everything and visit him when she was older and had a pickup of her own. Maybe she would be married and have twins by then.

Suddenly the plane rocked hard and an angry voice yelled as the door flew open. Sara jerked back in the seat as a hairy arm reached across her lap and snapped the key to off. The green lights on the dash turned black.

"Damn you girls," a voice said. "I'll have the sheriff on you two." The barn was half-dark, but Sara could see Deanie turn as white as one of the clouds she had just dreamed.

Deanie half-fell out of her side of the plane and took off running for her bike with the man right behind. Sara jumped down and went the other way, then circled back behind the barn for her bicycle. She could see Deanie, pedaling hard, disappear down the road.

The man strode back all red-faced and out of breath. Sara couldn't make herself run, and started to cry. The man stood over her for a minute, his chest rising and falling like it was going to burst. Then he waved his arm. "Aw, go on," he said. "But if I ever spot you around here again I'll have the sheriff lock you up for good! You understand?"

Sara could only nod.

"Now go on! Git!"

Sara found Deanie waiting behind Side's Store, smoking a cigarette. "I could have flown it, Sara. You know I nearly did. I nearly really flew a real airplane."

At Deanie's Uncle Porter had printed a message on a tablet by the phone. "SARA—BEN RAY SAYS YOU CAN COME ON HOME."

It was dark when Sara got to her house. The light from the TV flashed and Ben Ray was propped up on the sofa watching. He was alone.

"There's some pizza in the oven, Pumpkin." He didn't look up. Sara stood there, watching. It was a movie she had seen before, and she knew what would happen, but she didn't move until a commercial came on. She wanted Ben Ray to say something, anything, about Bubble Head. But he didn't.

"You and Deanie have fun?" Ben Ray asked. He still didn't look at Sara. "What'd you do?"

Sara knew that Ben Ray wouldn't really want to know what they did. "We just flew around here and there," she said.

The commercial was over and the movie started again.

"That's nice," Ben Ray said, still staring straight ahead. The glow from the TV washed across his face and Sara thought he looked happy.

Sara started toward the kitchen. "Bring me another slice when you come, will you, Pumpkin?"

Sara stayed in the kitchen a long time. She turned out the light and ate by the glow from the streetlamp. When she finally went back in the living room Ben Ray was asleep. Something different was on the TV, a new movie, one she had never seen before, and she sat down to watch it closely, to see what might happen next.

The Way the Big World Is

I GOT my first job on my twelfth birthday. Some of that day I'm sure about but can't really remember, like my mother baking a cake for me, for she always did. And like my father being there, singing along on "Happy Birthday" in his usual way, and even now, thirty years later, I can hear his voice, but whether from that day or another I can't know.

What I remember most is the phone call my father answered. Above all the confusion I heard him say, I'm sure Bobby would, and yes, I'll tell him, and yes, he'll be ready in the morning, and all at once I had a summer job, a real one.

My mother woke me the next morning at five, as she did every morning but Sundays for the next few weeks of that early summer. This, so that I was ready when a half hour later a Borden's milk truck groaned to a stop out front. I raced out into the coolness of the dark morning and with one awkward giant step propelled myself up into the cab of the truck and onto the blue patterned seat.

"Rolly Chaney," the driver said and took my hand firmly in his. I told him my name, then cleared my throat and squeezed back the best I could, the way my father had taught me to shake hands. He studied me a minute and I straightened, trying to look taller. I tensed my left arm, hoping he would notice my muscle.

"Hell, boy, do this," he said, and I looked up at Rolly Chaney's broad face that glowed yellow in the light of the cab.

"Do like this," he said again, and I watched while he ran his fat red tongue back and forth at the corner of his mouth.

"You dribbled all night," he said, and laughed. Then he lifted one of his hips and farted.

I did what he said. Licked the corners of my mouth, feeling the roughness of dried saliva with my tongue, then rubbed my mouth with my palm and wiped it on my jeans.

Rolly held a newspaper across the steering wheel as he maneuvered the truck out toward the edge of town, headed for Eustace and Mabank and Kemp and Three Points, headed for the smattering of cafes and drive-ins and tiny markets that dotted that part of East Texas. He drove with the cab light on, his big head bobbing up and down between the news and the highway, and by the time we got to the first stop he had tossed the paper, one section at time, to the black-matted floor under my feet.

As he drove Rolly held two pints of chocolate milk between his thighs, and in a minute he handed me one of them. "Well, drink it, boy. Two things about chocolate milk. One it's free, and two it'll make your pecker grow." He laughed an enormous laugh, the bottles in the back clanking and jangling as if on cue.

We made our stops, and after a couple of days it was routine, pulling up to the back doors of cafes, moving through kitchens that smelled of bacon grease, easing past bubbling pots of blackeyed peas. Negro women peeled potatoes and chopped onions and opened giant green-labeled tins of stewed tomatoes. Rolly mostly talked with the owners, shooting the shit, he called it, or flirted with a waitress if she was young.

I counted inventory, filling a wooden crate with expired bottles and empties, and straightened up the coolers, making room for so many fresh bottles, which I checked off just like Rolly had taught me. Then straining my skinny arms, I hauled in jugs of sweet milk, with cream, thick and golden on the top, and quarts of buttermilk, seeping with a familiar sourness, and my favorites, those slender pints of chocolate milk. I snapped open coolers that held smoked hams and extra hamburger and round hard heads of cabbage. Out behind the markets the smells of black bananas and mushy lettuce and cardboard buckets of entrails from the butcher. All that clanking and counting and carrying and smelling and then into the cab and dozing off and waking again as Rolly shook me back from some forgotten dream and I'd stumble out again at the next stop.

We had twenty-three customers over seven or eight hours, along a route that took us past peanut fields and tomato patches and sandy hills strewn with yellow-bellied watermelons, a looping route that took us in a wandering circle around the little town that for me was home.

Between stops, Rolly asked me questions. "You getting any nooky?" he asked, and I looked straight ahead, not knowing exactly what he meant but knowing it was a word I wouldn't try out on my mother over supper. "We need to get you some nooky, boy. There's nothing to it. You pay attention to old Rolly and you'll see." He watched me a minute, waiting for my reaction.

A cat raced across the road almost under the front wheels of the truck, but Rolly didn't brake or veer or even flinch. "Just another pussy, boy. Plenty of pussy in the world." He glanced in the rearview mirror and I waited for his reaction, afraid to look back. "You like the way pussy looks, hot shot? You ever see a pussy, boy?"

I shook my head and held my arm out the window of the truck, tilting my hand up and then down, feeling my arm rise and fall with the hot push of the wind.

"Open that up," he said, and pointed to the closed glove compartment in front of me. "Go ahead."

I pushed the silver button and the door snapped open.

"See that book?" he asked.

"Uh-huh," I said.

"Well, look at it, boy. Hold it up and flip it with your thumb."

I took the book out. It was thick, its edges blackened and warped. I flipped through it awkwardly once and then again.

"You like that?" he asked. His face was flushed, redder than his orange hair. "You like that?" he asked again, his voice hard and soft all at once, like a rubber hammer pounding on a tin roof.

I shook my head, knowing I was lying, and shoved the book back in its dark place, not daring to look his way, tilting my head to the side to let the wind whip through my hair, through my ears, drowning out all other sounds.

We pulled in behind City Market, next to an empty pickup that was backed up tight against a loading chute. With relief I jumped down from the cab, but Rolly told me to stay there for a minute. I started to climb back into the shade of the cab and thought about the book, the women's nipples, their legs spread wide; women with hard, thin lips molded into painful smiles. But I was chicken. If Rolly caught me in the cab I knew he would ride me forever, so I scooped up a handful of the thousands of bottle caps that covered the back lot, and with a sidearm motion sailed them in one gentle curve after another towards a smoking trash barrel that stood in the open ground.

"Hot shot. Hey. Come here." Rolly was holding open the back screen door with one foot and motioning for me to come. He had a blank look on his face and I wondered if something was wrong, if I had left the old milk in the cooler last time.

The back room of the market was dark, the walls wobbly lines of brick. Crates and boxes were stacked haphazardly at one end. A bare bulb hung still and yellow from the ceiling. The concrete floor gleamed through a scattering of sawdust. The far side of the room was made into a pen, with runs of pipe that stretched up higher than my head. A red steer panted in one corner of the pen and at the other end a Negro man smoked a cigarette and studied the animal through heavy-lidded eyes. He cocked his head toward Rolly, who grinned and said, "Okay, Moon, go ahead."

Moon tossed his cigarette to the sawdust floor and ground it out with the toe of his rubber boot. Moon turned and stopped a moment, watching me, then wiped his hands on the front of his apron, and I backed up a step or two. I looked toward the doorway that led to the market and then at Rolly, but he just shook his head, the grin still tight across his face.

When I looked back Moon had a rifle halfway to his shoulder and was maneuvering around the wary steer. Then all at once he pulled the gun up and tight, and the scream of the rifle and one harsh bellow echoed together. Then Moon was on the steer. He pulled a chain down from a pulley, and with a quick wrap and a twist and a couple of jerks the steer was suspended by its hind legs, turning slowly, a neat hole in one side of its head and a red, raw wound opposite. From a leather scabbard under his apron Moon pulled a thin-bladed knife, long and slightly curved. With an effortless motion he cut across the steer's neck, releasing a dark red stream that drained into a bucket he kicked into place.

Moon stepped back and for a second or two admired his work in much the same satisfied way my father surveyed a field he had just mowed. Then from a cross brace on the wall Moon took a malt cup and held it under the still-flowing stream until it overflowed. He lifted the cup to his lips and took an exaggerated gulp and made an audible smack, looking at Rolly and then at me, a grin taking up the bottom of his face. He held the cup out.

"Come on, boy," he said, "this'll put iron in you, make you a man." Rolly gave me a little shove, his hand on my belt, but I twisted away and backed against the wall. I planted my feet wide, digging into the sweet give of the sawdust. Rolly took the cup from Moon, and pushed it toward my face, hooting and snorting, blood splashing everywhere. Then the room tilted to one side, and everything went blank.

Later that afternoon we pulled into the A&W where Rolly eased the cab of the truck under the metal awning. He called the flat-chested car hop honey and darling and, cocking his head my way, said, "Now hot shot here, he has what a girl like you needs." She laughed, and I made myself small next to the door.

Rolly kept a bottle of whiskey under the seat. The whiskey was for afternoons only, after the last delivery. He ordered me a root beer, one that came in a megaphone-shaped cup with foam swirled across the top. He got a tall Coke with ice, then topped it off with a healthy splash of whiskey. He always did this. Then he took a sip, gave a little shudder, and pushed the bottle my way. "Here, hot shot," he said, "this'll put some lead in your pencil."

I shook my head and picked at flecks of steer blood that had dried black on my jeans. I knew I was a big disappointment.

"Hell, boy," he said, "you'll never be a man."

"Yes, sir," I said, figuring he had me pegged. We sat there forever, it seemed, before he started the truck and pulled out on the highway.

Then right out of the blue, right when I thought I might make it home in silence, he said, "I know a neighbor of yours."

"You do?" I asked. "Which one? Snyder?"

"Not him. Hell, no. Snyder's an asshole."

That puzzled me. Snyder was my favorite. When he wasn't fishing, Snyder worked in town, at Carson's hardware store on the square, and spent hours with me comparing the virtues of Hula Poppers and Devil's Horses and deep-running River Runts. Sometimes he would meet me late afternoon at Barron's Lake and I'd watch while he stood at the flat end of his johnboat and demonstrated the action of each type, with luck pulling in a redear or a goggle-eye in the process. Snyder was small, but tough as a rope. His wrist flicked a bamboo rod as if it were an extension of his arm.

"Nell's who I know," Rolly said, not looking at me, staring straight through the bug-splattered windshield with a funny grin on his face. "Not Snyder," he said with disgust. "Nell. You ask her sometime what she thinks of Rolly Chaney. Not in front of Snyder though—he wouldn't go for that. But you ask her."

I would never have a reason to talk to Snyder's wife, and besides, I only saw her spinning around town in that new station wagon of hers that said "Estate" in fancy chrome letters on the back. My mother didn't think much of Nell, probably because she dyed her hair red and wore bright clothes, but all she ever said was some comment about poor Mr. Snyder, wanting a pickup to haul his fishing boat around in and Nell browbeating him until she got that station wagon.

That evening I sat at the kitchen table, carving the bottom out of the A&W megaphone with a butcher knife. I had a whole stack of them by then. My mother sat across from me, small and straight against a ladder-back chair. She held a pan in her lap, snapping and stringing green beans, watching me, like she was waiting for the knife to slice my finger to the bone. For a long time she was quiet. I could tell something was on her mind. "Is Mr. Chaney a nice man?" she finally asked.

"Uh-huh," I said, not looking up.

"Does he have a foul mouth, son?"

"I don't know," I said, but right away knew that wasn't a good answer. She waited, so I said, "Well, maybe sometimes, I guess."

My father sat in the next room, listening, I knew. I could smell his pipe, hear him draw on it, an occasional soft suck followed by a mellow pop.

My mother placed the pan on the table and, carrying her apron bunched with one hand, moved to the door where she could see both me and my father.

"Lamb?" she asked, softly. She never raised her voice, just moved it along some invisible scale of intensity. "Did you hear what Bobby said?" I didn't hear an answer. Then she said, "It's just as I suspected. Mr. Chaney has a foul mouth."

Then I heard my father, his voice with an irritated edge. "Mother," he said, "the boy's growing up. The work force is that way and he might as well learn it now. That's the way the big world is."

"You know Mr. Chaney is not a Christian," she said.

"None of my business," he said. "None at all."

"Well, where Bobby works is," she said, and my father didn't answer. My mother stood there a moment, but all I heard was the suck and pop of his pipe again, this time a little faster. My mother came over to me and put her hand on my shoulder. She looked down. Her eyes glistened. She shook her head like she knew everything I did, everything I thought. Like the way I flipped through Rolly's girlie book when I was alone in the truck, like the way I wanted to sip his whiskey and laugh at his dirty jokes. Like the way I wanted to be a man. I could feel a whole life of guilt stretching out before me, filled with girls and then women, and cussing and whiskey, then a whole stream of other unimaginable sins, all performed with my mother standing silently over me, shaking her head.

After a while my mother moved out to the backyard. I

poured a glass of milk, stuck the megaphone on my arm, wearing it like a wrist guard, and started toward my room. My father stopped me as I walked by. "Son," he said, "just do what Mr. Chaney says and mind your own business. You owe the man an honest day's work and that's all. You understand?"

"Uh-huh. Yes, sir," I said, and went to my room. I lay on my bed until my mother called me for supper, maneuvering my two favorite model planes above me in a deadly series of dogfights.

Three weeks passed. Three weeks of stumbling around in the dark, pulling on a white T-shirt and jeans and black basketball shoes, then jolting off into the morning, watching the sun push a thin streak of light into the early sky. Bouncing along with the smell of Rolly's first cigar, remembering to wipe the smears of chocolate milk from my lips. I soaked up more of Rolly's stories, filling my head with fuzzy images of women begging for it, of California where he would soon make it big, stories of the moneyed boys who were either born with a silver spoon or were a bunch of crooks. Rolly waved his big freckled arm in the hot air, pointing out the way things were from behind the wheel of the milk truck.

One sweltering Friday afternoon we pulled into the A&W and Debbie, the carhop, came out to take our order. Her breasts would never be gigantic, but with Rolly's guidance I began to appreciate the mysteries of her ass. I watched Debbie prance away, scribbling on a pad, then sticking the stub of a pencil into her hair where miraculously it stayed.

Then Rolly said, "Well, I'll be damned. Look at that, will you."

I moved forward and, sitting on the edge of the seat, could see past Rolly to the far side of the parking lot where a station wagon gleamed in the sun: Nell's, but she wasn't in it.

Rolly looked back at the shade of the building where Debbie sat, alone, flipping through a magazine, a cigarette to one side. Then I felt Rolly stiffen. "What the hell," he said, and sat upright, pressed back against the seat.

I looked past him. Snyder stood there, not ten feet away from Rolly's door. Rolly leaned forward then and swelled up in a way I'd never seen. He looked down on Snyder like a bear from a tree. I couldn't see Rolly's face, but I could hear his short breaths sucking in the still air.

"There's lots better places than this town to peddle milk," Snyder said.

Rolly bent forward and faked a cough. He covered his mouth with his left hand and with his right pulled a revolver, squat and black, from beneath the seat. It looked like a toy and I thought this was another of Rolly's jokes. But then I sensed the gun's weight, how heavy it sank into his hand. From my side of the truck I could just see Snyder's head. Looking down at him that way, he seemed even smaller, and his hair lay like thin copper strands combed across his head. His eyes were heavy and dark with their own clouds. He was sweating and Rolly was sweating and so was I.

"You hear me?" Snyder asked. "Find another place to peddle your goddamn milk."

"Maybe I will, maybe I won't," Rolly said. "I like it here. Seems about right to me."

"You stay here and it won't be," Snyder said. He turned sideways and glanced back at the Estate wagon parked at the edge of the lot, and I wondered about Nell, where she was, why Snyder wasn't driving his beat-up Chevy.

Snyder looked back at Rolly and I saw him grow, moving to the truck, stretching up. He put one hand on the door for balance and I lifted my hand in a little wave, but he never took his eyes off Rolly.

"Get your goddamned hand off my truck," Rolly said, and tightened his grip on the gun. I reached for the door handle, but without looking Rolly touched my leg with the barrel and I froze. The sourness of root beer and milk rose up in my throat and bubbled in my mouth.

Then Snyder said, "Don't be in town tomorrow. I'm not telling you again. You here tomorrow and you'll be sucking on my 30.06. You understand?"

"Careful what you say, little man," Rolly said and raised his gun up, just enough so that Snyder could see it.

Snyder jerked back, but his face stayed the same, maybe a little whiter. "A popgun like that'll get you in big trouble," he said, then half turned and started moving back to his car, where I figured his rifle was. Rolly must have guessed it, too.

"Hey, hold on a minute," Rolly said, and I saw a strain come across his face. His shirt was soaked and stuck to his belly. He tapped the gun lightly on the seat.

Snyder stopped for a minute and waited, but Rolly had run out of words so Snyder started toward his car again, this time almost running.

All at once I saw myself like in a movie, grabbing the gun, locking on to Rolly's arm until Snyder got away, saving his life. But I couldn't move.

Then everything stopped, became still, and all at once I could see myself, as if from above, as if I had left my body and was soaring in a high, tight circle like a hawk eyeing the ground. Looking down I could see Snyder, small, moving alone across the hot asphalt. And I could see myself, also small, but with Rolly.

Then I raised myself up, one knee on the seat. "Snyder," I shouted. "Don't go. Wait for me."

"You little bastard," Rolly said. "If you get out of this truck, that's it."

Snyder stopped. He turned and started back toward the truck. I put my hand on the door handle, but my arm wouldn't work, like it wasn't my arm at all.

Without looking, Rolly punched me with the gun and said, "Get out!" Then he said, "You never were worth a damn, anyhow."

I still couldn't move.

"Goddammit, boy, I said get out." Rolly moved the gun to his left hand and started the engine. Then Snyder started running towards us, like he could stop the truck.

Rolly reached across and pushed my door open. He gave me a shove, and I tried to scramble out but slipped on the paper beneath my feet and tumbled to the asphalt.

The truck rolled back, its gears grinding, then lurched heavily forward. Snyder started after the truck, but only for a few steps before he stopped. Without a look my way, without even one word, he turned and left, the station wagon quiet and smooth as it dipped out of the parking lot, then screeching off down the road.

My elbow was badly scraped and dripping blood. Debbie brought me a wet napkin. "You need a ride?" she asked. "I'll call for you."

I dabbed at my elbow without looking up. I wasn't ready to go or see anyone. "My mom's in town," I lied. "I can find her."

I walked to the edge of the asphalt and started collecting megaphone cups that had blown against the chain link fence. For a few minutes I practiced what I would tell my father, the truth at first, and then all sorts of lies. Nothing seemed to work.

Once I looked back at Debbie. She seemed to glow, leaning against the side of the building. I almost could see her breasts rise and fall as she breathed.

I gathered a wobbly tower of cups and then placed them one at a time, their open ends down, in a line that stretched across the smooth black lot. Then I stomped the first one. It flattened, crumpled, turned to one side. I felt tears roll down my face, but I kept on, stomping the next one and then the next one, harder and harder, faster and faster. Finally, with all my strength I hit one perfectly with the flat of my heel, straight down and centered. It popped loud, exploded almost like a firecracker.

For a while I watched the late afternoon traffic go by, thinking that a car would pull in and it would be Snyder, but that didn't happen.

I walked home slowly that evening and it was nearly dark when I got there. My mother asked if anything was wrong, was I all right. I said no, nothing was wrong, and yes, I was all right, and went to my room.

After a while my father came in and I told him everything—about Rolly and the girlie book and the cup of steer blood and about the gun and Snyder and Nell. He listened quietly, sometimes nodding, sometimes shaking his head. After he left I could hear his voice, and then my mother's, and then I fell asleep.

It was dark when my mother came in carrying a tray of food, and I could tell she had been crying. She stood there a minute like she wanted to ask me something, and I felt like I needed to explain myself, but I couldn't.

From the living room I heard my father's voice, asking if anyone had seen his glasses. It was so quiet I could hear him scraping out his pipe with a knife.

My mother put down the tray and moved to the door. Then she turned. "Just because tomorrow is Saturday," she said, "don't think you can sleep late. There's plenty of work to be done around here."

She closed the door softly, and I was glad to be alone.

Caddo

From the dock just at dark, Brian picked up the distant chug of his brother's boat as it moved toward him across the still water. Then quickly, before Carter could spot him, Brian moved silently back up the slope away from the lake. He passed under the looming shadows of cypress trees, then quickened his pace when he crossed the rectangles of light thrown onto the grass through the windows of the cabins that lined the shore.

This was their second day at Slagle's Cabins. The sign out front read "Kitchenettes, Boat Dock, Bait." Nothing fancy, built in the thirties, not even a phone in the office. An old black man was waiting when they walked in the door. He couldn't find the key for their cabin but said that didn't matter.

"I keeps my eye on things. Don't you worry none. We clean the cabins and change the sheets when you leave, and don't bother you none while you here. That's the way it's been for fifty-seven years, so don't figure on no change."

While they signed the register Leroy kept talking. "You boys sure should of been here last week. Last week or next week. Yassuh, last week them crappie was spawning up in the shallows. The fellas that had your cabin caught a boat full."

Carter snickered. "Probably from Dallas. Fishing with minnows, I bet."

"Yassuh, with minnows. They sure caught themselves a boat full."

"Why next week?" Brian asked, and Leroy looked at him quizzically. "You said we should have been here last week for the crappie. Either that or next week. What's the deal with next week?"

"Oh, sure nuf that's right. Me and my grandson, Merle, he's up from Houston, got a inside job at the big lumber yard there, he's gonna help me put up TV antennas on all the cabins. Yassuh, by next week you could of had TV from all over."

March was the only time to fish Caddo Lake, a natural crater of water that spread thinly across the northeast Texas border and into Louisiana. By April the water plants, the hyacinths and lilies and moss, reached up through the blackness of the water and touched the surface. Then motors churned and fouled on their tentacles, and green slime coated artificial lures. In March the mosquitoes had started, but their drones hadn't yet filled the night and the air cooled quickly after dark so that to sleep the two brothers could take refuge under the worn sheets of their cots.

When they were growing up Carter fished the stock ponds and creeks and rivers around their East Texas home. He was older than Brian by five years and until he got his license at sixteen the two boys bicycled off together with their silver Zebco 33's and a box tangled with bright Hula Poppers and sparkling Devil's Horses and double-spinner yellow-tailed H&H's. They almost always brought the fish home. Mostly stringers full of bluegills and goggle-eye perch and, if they were lucky, a large-mouth bass or two.

Their Dad would pull on his pipe and watch while the boys gutted and scaled and argued over who had caught what. Carter always caught the most and the biggest fish, and it seemed to Brian that their Dad always liked that and gave Carter his silent approval. Now Brian thought of fish guts every time he caught a whiff of Prince Albert tobacco and thought of pipe smoke and his dad every time he smelled fish.

From the cabin's porch Brian heard Carter kill the little three-and-a-half-horse Johnson. Then the faint scrape of a paddle against the aluminum boat followed by a gentle thud as the boat nosed in to the dock. Brian waited a minute, not to appear too anxious, then switched on the outside light and stepped off the porch and made his way slowly back down to the edge of the lake.

By flashlight they cleaned the half-dozen small bass that Carter had strung, rinsing blood and scales from their hands in the cool water. They pitched the entrails and heads into the shallow water down and away from the dock for the turtles and cottonmouths to divvy up in their mysterious ways.

"First time I came over here," Carter said, "a crowd of little rug-headed pickaninnies would have swamped the boat, wanting to clean your fish for a dollar." While Carter talked he wiped his knife dry on the leg of his jeans and snapped it shut. He stared out over the dark lake. "Then they got big ideas and moved off to Shreveport and Longview where they could get real money. Betcha half of 'em are on welfare today. They didn't know they were living in paradise."

"Hey," Brian said, slapping at his neck, "mosquitoes are

about to carry me off. Let's get to the cabin." The last thing Brian wanted was to talk race relations with his brother.

They walked in silence back toward the cabin, Carter leading the way with the bundle of dripping fish, Brian carrying his brother's rod and reel.

"What were they hitting?" Brian finally asked.

"Nothing for a while," Carter said. "Then I tied up the boat and waded back into a little inlet. You know, you can walk all over this damned lake."

"Except for the holes," Brian said.

Carter ignored him. "I could hardly cast for the brush, but for about ten minutes, when it got still right before dark, it didn't seem to matter. They would have hit a kitchen fork. You should have gone with me."

"Tomorrow. We'll go early," Brian said. "I have this paper due on Tuesday, you know, and in grad school they play hardball."

"So you sat in the cabin and read? With all this lake and God only knows how many fish waiting for you? You book-boys will never learn."

Brian laughed, but it wasn't easy. He could feel the bite in Carter's voice.

Carter flopped the fish in the sink. He rested both hands wide on the counter top, his arms stiff, his head bowed over the sink like he was about to throw up. After a minute, though, he turned his head towards Brian and grinned. "Let's freeze 'em, impress the women when we get home. Okay?"

Brian nodded, glad that Carter had shaken the beginnings of one of his black moods.

"Hand me a beer will you, little brother? Or while you're at it, hand me two."

After Carter had cleaned up they walked the quarter mile to eat at Haddad's. Above them tree frogs fussed and courted and jeered. It was Saturday night, but the place was empty except for the waitress and a black cook in the kitchen. The brothers scarfed down platters of fried catfish with hushpuppies and mounds of help-yourself cole slaw. Carter smothered his with Louisiana hot sauce.

Brian felt good to be fishing with Carter again. It had been five or six years; he couldn't remember the last time. Just four days ago Brian had come home for spring break and over a piece of their mama's lemon icebox pie Carter suddenly looked away from his Sunday afternoon dose of the Spurs and said, "Brian, let's go to Caddo for a couple or three days."

At that, Jerri, Carter's wife, gave a big snort from across the room. She did everything—taught junior high and ran their eight- and ten-year-olds back and forth everywhere and fed everybody.

Carter had slowly turned to face Jerri. "Now, in a couple of months you'll have all summer off." Carter spoke softly, which surprised Brian. "And my brother and me, we're way behind in our fishing." With that he reached over and patted Brian on the shoulder and sank right back into the basketball game.

Carter took a two-day leave from his sales job at the True Value; he was their sporting goods specialist and a valued employee, so that was no problem. Jerri was another story. Twelve years of Carter and two kids, she openly described her life as a plate of burnt toast. Right up to the time they left she pouted and smoked and stewed. Finally Carter grabbed Brian by the arm and they just drove off. "Guess she'll be here when we get back," he joked.

But Brian got the idea neither of them gave a big damn. Ornery had just become an ordinary way of being.

They had pulled Carter's little fourteen-foot johnboat and trailer two hours northeast. Brian felt an exhilaration at first, like he was ten again and going off to fish strange waters with his big brother. But ninety miles and a few beers later, as Carter smoked and talked, an uneasiness that rode with them finally chipped the mood away, and by the time they arrived Brian felt empty.

Somehow it wasn't the same. In fact, as he remembered it, everything had changed when Carter turned sixteen and got his own car. It was as if from that day on he had sped away and out of Billy's life, finding another world of girls and cars and beer. They still fished a weekend now and then, but the quarry had changed. "How many fish?" had been changed into "How many beers?" and "How many different girls?" Finally, Brian stopped going with him and grew up mostly alone, the twin bed across from Brian's either empty or sagging with a Carter who slept with his back to his brother.

"So, tell me about the university." Carter had a pile of bones and a scattering of empties in front of him. He moved the beer bottles around as he talked, as if they had strings attached and he could tie them in knots. He always had a cigarette lit, but it seemed more just something to do than to smoke.

Brian didn't like to talk about Austin and UT—at least not to Carter. About his enthusiasm, his effort to describe the magic that swept over him when he had first lost himself in Robert Penn Warren and Walker Percy, and then in Richard Hugo. He wanted to read a Hugo poem to Carter, make him feel the power in those simple words that described an ordinary softball game. Yeah, he thought, a poem about men just like Carter, men with ordinary jobs and ordinary, mostly unhappy wives, men drinking beer and telling bad jokes simply playing a softball game, but reaching for something more. And probably coming up a little hung over and empty. But Brian knew that Carter would never listen, that he would only laugh. And maybe it was silly for grown men to be excited by such things.

So Brian talked about football, the Longhorns' prospects for the fall, how the baseball team had swept an early series on the road.

"The pros will raid 'em," Carter said in a conspiratorial whisper. "They have a good year and the pros will pick 'em clean. The niggers 'specially. They know they can't make their grades, shouldn't be there anyhow. They'll offer big bucks and take them in a hurry." He leaned back then and nodded, satisfied with his analysis.

Brian's mind raced through several counters to Carter's redneck opinion, wanting his brother's words to simply go away but feeling too guilty, too angry inside to ignore them. Why does Carter have to still be this way? he thought. It's 1994 and there's my brother with a Jefferson Davis mind.

But before Brian could respond Carter changed the subject. "You found a woman down there? I hear there's lots of free-love women in Austin. But that AIDS thing has slowed them down more than a little bit, I bet."

There *was* a woman and Brian wanted to tell Carter about her, but didn't. He dreaded the day they might meet. Carter wouldn't go for a bushy-hair-under-the-arms kind of woman like Rebecca. And Rebecca, when Brian talked about Carter, just shook her head and asked in disbelief, "And you're brothers?"

But Carter wasn't really asking about the possibility of Brian having a woman. He wouldn't really want to hear about that. He just wanted to talk about women.

"You gonna use it nowadays, you better put it in a bag," he said. "I'll tell you that much."

Then a couple of black men came in, talking loud and joking with the cook. Carter pushed back from the table and slipped a dollar under a bottle. "Wouldn't have seen *that* ten years ago. I'll tell you that, too."

The two black men took a booth in the corner and Brian saw that one of them was Leroy, the custodian at Slagle's Cabins. While Carter paid, Leroy spotted Brian and motioned him to come over. He introduced his grandson, Merle. The fellow looked like he might have played defensive end for the Oilers and Brian felt his own hand get lost in Merle's big handshake.

Leroy went on about some bloodbait that was surefire for channel cats. Then he held up a glow-in-the-dark plastic worm with spinners and double hooks. This was surefire, too. Merle appeared not too interested; he seemed annoyed that his granddaddy would be going out of his way to give fishing tips to a white man.

Carter waited across the room. One foot propped open the screen door. He chewed on a toothpick. Brian motioned to his brother to come over. He held up the plastic worm. "Leroy says this is what they're hitting." But Carter just gave the two black men a little nod and stepped out into the night.

"You should have come over," Brian said as they headed down the dark road that led to the cabin. "Leroy just might be right. He's been around this lake a long time, you know."

"Yeah," Carter said. "He might be right, but that big bad dude of a grandson gave me the creeps. Did you see the way he stared at you? Wouldn't want to run into him out here alone. That's for damn sure."

"Oh, come on, Carter. Just because the man is black and happens to be big doesn't make him a 'bad dude.'"

Carter didn't answer, but even in the dark Brian felt his brother's smirk.

Brian sat alone on the porch steps while Carter busied himself inside, sorting through his tackle box and sipping on beers. The breeze had picked up from across the lake and kept the mosquitoes pretty much away, but when it died it left a staleness that seemed to be centuries old. The cabin finally went dark, but Brian waited until much later before he slipped back inside and into bed.

Caddo is more a maze of waist-deep boatways cut out of the cypress than it is a real lake. Early morning fog hangs head-high and filters the sun, giving everything an eerie glow.

The leaves are too green, the water too black, the flutter of birds too bright.

Carter pushed the boat quietly down one of the cuts, and then another. The brothers fell into an unspoken rhythm. Carter sat in the stern and worked the trolling motor with his knee. He systematically cast back and to his left, dropping his lure inches from stumps and brush piles, reading the lake's silky surface, the way the minnows raced, always alert to the still water, the way it rippled and pooled. Brian worked the opposite side and the front. He had brought his old Pony League cap and as the sun got higher pulled it tighter above his eyes. He watched Carter change baits, starting out with topwaters and as the morning progressed trying spinners and finally a deep-running River Runt. But the spinners came back smothered with moss, and he hung a submerged log and had to cut away the River Runt.

Carter had a couple of decent strikes and landed a crappie, eating size if you had a half-dozen more to go with it. He gently slid it back into the water and watched it wiggle slowly away. "Grow up, baby, grow up," he almost whispered.

Brian had gotten discouraged and arm-weary and for a while just sat and watched a gathering of herons fuss at the end of a sandbar.

"Damned moss," Carter said, whipping the end of his rod. He had reeled in a wad of green that hid his lure. "Let's find some deeper water." He jerked the motor into life and they chugged off to the east where a flat area of water lay like an open bay in the overgrown lake.

The water was deeper and they both tried first this and then that kind of midrunner. "This water just cries out for yellow lures," Carter said. "Something the damned bass can see."

On his third cast Brian felt his lure jerk to a halt. No give at all. Carter saw him strain back on the rod and shook his head. "You hung yourself a stump, little brother. This is a topwater lake," he said, reeling in his line. "We might as well go back for some cold beer and try again late."

Just then Brian felt some give and his line moved across to the left and then straight toward him. The breeze had picked up out of the south and he thought it might be some kind of illusion, but Carter saw it, too, and leaned forward, rocking the little boat, his rod clattering against metal as he let it drop.

Brian worked the fish back and forth, the drag on his reel screaming each time it made a run. "That's no bass," Carter shouted. "It would have broke water long ago."

Sure enough, when Brian finally maneuvered the fish next to the boat it wasn't a bass, but huge and speckled, four or five feet long, with a mouthful of teeth that worked at the lure lodged in the corner of its jaw.

"A damned alligator gar," Carter's voice was a mixture of disgust and awe. "Look at the size of that sucker."

"You want me to bring him in?" Brian asked, hoping Carter would reach over with his knife and cut the line, let the monster have the lure. Brian knew that a fish that size in their little boat would be a dangerous mix.

Then a single blast rocked Brian to the bone. He jerked around. Carter still had a pistol aimed at the gar, which now was slowly turning belly-up. The dark water turned pink and then crimson, as if a bottle of red ink had spilled over the side of the boat.

Carter nodded to himself with satisfaction. Then, when he saw the look on Brian's face, he said, "One like that, he'll eat hundreds, maybe thousands of fingerling bass a year." Carter looked at the sky, where a dark cloud churned toward them, eating away the blue, and without a word pointed up and started the engine. He slipped his pistol back in the tackle box and handed Brian his knife. "Cut away." Brian cut the line and the bow lifted as they moved off.

By the time they got to the dock, hard drops of rain splattered the water and twanged the floor of the metal boat. They grabbed their gear and raced to the cabin.

"Whoo-ee, that could have got bad," Carter said. He washed his hands slowly at the kitchen sink, then found some bologna and cheese and mayonnaise in the refrigerator. He set a cold six-pack of beer on the linoleum counter. By then the rain beat sideways against the windows. Brian turned on the lights and sat at the dinette in the middle of the room.

Carter opened two beers, put the sandwich stuff on the table, and joined him. Brian felt him looking his way, but he kept staring at the rain.

"Something wrong, partner?" Carter asked. "The ride back in a little rough? Had to move on, you know. Didn't want to get caught out there in this. That's for sure."

"Did you have to shoot the gar?" Brian turned and looked across the glare of the table at his brother. "Why couldn't you just cut him loose, let him go?"

Carter stared at the tabletop. He fiddled with the package of bologna, giving it little spins on the slick surface. "You have got soft, haven't you? I told you. Those damn gar'll eat more fish in a year than we could catch in a lifetime."

"There's lots of fish in the lake. Enough for us all."

"Well, where are they then, hot shot?" Carter's voice got a hint of shrillness and his face turned dark. He took three big swallows of beer.

"Do you always carry a gun?" Brian asked. "When did that start?"

"You've been in that ivory tower too long, little brother. East Texas's not like it was ten years ago. What you gonna do when you get out? When you have to make it in the real world?"

"Teach, I guess."

"Teach, huh. Well there's plenty of schools around home. Jerri's been doing it for years. I guess you could, too, if she can."

"That's not exactly what I have in mind," Brian said. "I mean it would be okay, I guess. But you know."

A look of disgust crossed Carter's face. "Yeah, I think I do know. You're too damn good to come back to East Texas, aren't you? Hell, I've got a job, I make it just fine. What's wrong with that?"

"Nothing. Nothing's *wrong* with anything. You just shot that big old gar and I wondered why. I don't see killing anything you don't eat. That's all."

Carter walked over to the window. He stared out at the rain that had all but blown over. A few scattered drops still spat on the soft ground. "Ten years and look how you've changed. You're gonna turn hippie vegetarian if you don't get back up here pretty soon."

"No, Carter. It's not me. What happened to you? You were good in high school, made mostly A's, didn't you. A good enough halfback to play college ball."

"Junior college."

"Still, that's not bad. What happened? It seems as if you somehow got stuck fifteen years ago and never changed."

Carter wheeled around then, his back to the window. The sun had broken back through and the last drops of rain slid down the panes like tiny rainbow rivers. "What do you mean, what happened? Can't you see, can't you understand anything that's not in a damned book? I'm nineteen, I marry Jerri—you know you didn't just move in together back then, not around home you didn't, anyway—then the two kids. Hell, I had to get a job." Then he turned back to face the window. "Dammit, I do all right."

Just then, a crackling pop boomed through the air and a flash brighter than the sunlight streaked across the window. Carter jumped back as if he'd been shot, and the brothers stared at each other, frozen in place. For a few seconds the lights in the cabin darkened. The refrigerator went silent, then quickly resumed its monotonous whine. The lights flickered once, then stayed on.

"What the hell?" Carter asked, his voice barely a whisper.

"Lightning?" Brian speculated, not certain at all. Then a

low moan reached the cabin, the moan that would hang for years in the back of both men's minds.

They stepped out onto the porch. From there, two cabins up, they could see someone on the ground. Carter acted first. He hit the screen door with his fist and leaped out into the heavy afternoon air. Brian raced after him.

The moans were Leroy's. The old man hovered on the ground and rocked back and forth. His grandson Merle stretched out below him, his face slack, his arms and legs sprawled akilter like a broken puppet's. His chest was still. His hands were curled tight and the smell of scorched skin hung in the air. The mast for a TV antenna still sizzled on the grass beside him.

Brian started to ask the old man what had happened, but Carter pushed his pickup keys into Brian's hand and pointed at the power line drooping above them, connecting the main line to the cabin. "Go to Haddad's," he said. "Get some help." His voice was calm and firm, but Brian could see the panic in his eyes. Carter looked down at Merle, then pushed Leroy aside. The old man fell over and lay still, his eyes searching the sky for comfort.

Brian started for the pickup, running sideways, glancing back and then forward. Carter knelt over the stricken man. He put his head to Merle's chest and listened, then quickly tilted his chin back. Brian thought he hesitated just a moment, but it might have been only long enough to take a deep breath. Then, almost as if it were an act of love, Carter seized the big man's nose. His head dropped slowly down, and his mouth covered Merle's.

Brian waited at Haddad's for the ambulance. The cafe was thirteen miles from the nearest town. The waitress handed Brian a Coke while he paced, and refused his money. The whole world grew quiet and still.

The ambulance was a converted pickup with a camper top that rocked from side to side as it slid to a halt, its lights still dancing, the siren slowed to a small spinning sound. Brian led the way back to the lake, speed-shifting the pickup like he was a kid again.

A crowd had gathered. Voices hung quietly in the air. Nothing else had changed. Leroy still lay on the grass face up and prayed. Carter still moved above Merle, going from mouth to chest, his movements as strong and natural as those of some strange and absolutely free animal.

The medics knelt beside him. Quickly, blood pressure, then long moments with the stethoscope sliding across Merle's black chest. They motioned Carter aside, but he wouldn't stop. Brian could hear the rhythm of his brother's count. The medics' voices rose and finally Carter gave way; his back sagged with some secret weight. When he rose and turned his face was raw. It glistened with saliva and sweat and tears.

Brian watched as his brother moved slowly away, down to the edge of the lake. From there Carter stared out over the water, out over the play of minnows near the shore, out to where life still stirred and curled and flitted below the surface.

The Man Who
Talked to Houses

M Y NAME is Lyman Hendry. I'm sixty-one years old and my life has come down to realizing this: from the time a boy turns thirteen not a day passes that he doesn't think of sex, and when a man reaches sixty not a day passes that he doesn't think of death.

This is not a morbid preoccupation of mine; I don't turn to the obituaries first thing every morning, but I understand now why people do. It's not so much to see if anyone you know has kicked the bucket, or to gloat over outlasting some poor bastard who dropped over at fifty-two, or feeling off the hook when a Friday's average is eighty-seven and you figure that buys you twenty-six years more—it's not that at all, although honestly I've found myself playing out each of those games. No, it's just trying to figure what this death thing is all about, thinking maybe if you can figure that out then life won't be so damned much of a puzzle.

I live alone in a two-bedroom house in the middle of a

three-block dead-end street near the downtown section of this city. Nothing about the house is out of the ordinary—in the twenties this was the suburbs—and for the most part the houses for blocks around are simple stucco cottages. Young couples move in all starry-eyed and start pouring bucks into add-ons and slick kitchens and I ask them why bother, you could have a new house for the same money. But they just laugh. The rooms of the houses are small, and in my house the tile on the kitchen counter is the same green and white as that on the bathroom floor. For me that's okay, but if you're young just think of all the choices. I've lived here on this street for two-and-a-half years now, not because I particularly like it but because the rent is right and I've lost my reasons for moving. I have to live somewhere.

My neighbors have two big dogs, one a shepherd and one some shaggy north-country mixed breed who always looks hot and out of place. Through the chain link fence I see them scabbing the backyard, restless, digging here, rolling roughly there, pulling and shaking apart anything unlucky enough to fall within reach. A plastic ball or a rag doll has no chance at all. Despite an occasional night of barking I can't complain. I feel safe and don't have to worry that my neighbors will frown about the way I neglect my yard.

I'm alone a lot, most people would think I'm lonely, but I come from a string of single-child families so don't mind. It is something I'm used to, although for a few years being married changed that. I am the only child of parents who also were only children and my life followed the same pattern, my daughter Jenny being all I have. At thirty-eight she is still not a mother and has changed husbands three times in an effort, I like to think, to correct this injustice. A grandson would be nice, but for Jenny time seems to be running out. And although I try not to give it a thought anymore, sometimes I'm sad to think of the Hendrys tailing off this way.

For a lot of years Jenny and I lost contact. She was eight when her mama and I had our trouble. Doris, who was my

first and only wife, took Jenny to New Orleans and they settled into a life I couldn't know, and until Jenny reached her
twenties we were lost to each other. Since then, we got together once a few years back for an awkward lunch, followed
by a cycle of somewhat obligatory Christmas cards. Hers
with notes looped in a rush of red ink. Mine with a new re-
turn address each year.

I stayed on the move, following real estate booms from
place to place. Selling condos in San Diego and LA, pushing
developments in Aspen and Santa Fe, on to Denver during
the oil boom. There, with times being good I put a crew together and Hendry Homes moved a few spec houses. The
building I like, all of it: the design, the excitement when you
pour the slab, the smell of tar paper and pine resin. The selling afterwards I'm good at but find mostly a nuisance, wran-
gling over financing and carpet colors and garage door
openers.

When the market dropped I slid out of Denver and across
to Phoenix and ended up here in Tucson. When I sold out
in Phoenix I stuck my little chunk of cash in a long-term CD
and decided that was it. I always tried to shoot straight in
what can be a crooked business, and fell short a few times,
I'll admit, but not enough to wake me nights. I can start
pulling down a little social security check in a year, so I figure I've pretty well got it made if I watch my pennies.

Real estate's just another game and I got tired of playing.
But still I'm drawn to the way houses go up. Some nights I
drive out north into the foothills and park in the birth of a
raw subdivision and wander the streets. If no one's around I
talk to the houses, yellow skeletons in the night, waiting for
tomorrow. I shake my head over shortcuts taken, encourage
the slabs to be solid, the frames to be patient, remind them
of years still to come. Time enough for all things, I say, em-
barrassed then by the words that come from somewhere
deep, from my mother or some solemn pulpit I don't know.
Then I say it again, this time a little softer, time enough for

all things, and wonder for a while if saying it aloud makes it any less a lie.

Last year Jenny called from Houston and asked would I come for a visit. Right away I said sure—I had no reason not to—but the going was harder than the agreeing to go, and I found myself inventing excuses to stay here right up to the time I stepped on the plane.

Jenny showed me around Houston, trying to guess what I'd like. Most everything had changed, but we downed oysters at Captain Benny's and took in the Astros for a double-header. We talked some, mostly about this and that. I never asked about her mother, but right up front she said, "Mama's bitter and hard to be around." I didn't give a damn about Doris and hadn't for years, but Jenny went on in a fervent sort of confessional way, like she could mend things if they came out in the open. I told her what's past is history and might as well stay buried, but that didn't slow her. Jenny's big-boned but graceful, moves like some English actress I once saw on TV. Jenny talked and paced the room and something came over me that was hard to place. At first I thought it was guilt over the divorce and the way I had at the time run out on some responsibilities. Then I saw it wasn't that at all, but the way I was seeing Jenny for the first time as a woman no longer young. Little lines threaded around her mouth and at the corners of her eyes, and the skin under her arms sagged just a little. I felt sad for her and for me too, I guess.

She smoked and paced and talked for hours, tagging her latest ex-husband Mark the Shark and saying "no more, never again into the jaws of marriage." At that she laughed until she staggered from the room, and I heard her off and on in the bathroom for the next hour. Later she folded down the sofa for herself and gave me her bedroom. I tossed all night under lace-ruffled sheets.

On Sunday she took in church, which for her was unorthodox Eastern of some strange kind. I went along. There were black men in white robes, from Ethiopia she said, but they looked fifth ward Houston to me. I sat at the back and watched my daughter moving at ease among brass bells and incense burners, as serious as the flat-faced saints who stared down from the walls. On the way out we filed by the Miracle of Blood, peering down through a glass case that held a miniature picture of Christ on the cross. A few weeks before, according to the local priest, a red resinlike substance had appeared, oozing from Christ's punctured side. Even the local papers had covered it for a day or two. Later, Jenny asked me what I thought of it. I said there are some things you just can't explain and she let it go at that. But I thought that any God who busied himself with stuff like that sure must have run out of tricks, and probably went in for macrame, too.

A few months later when Jenny called and invited herself out—just for two or three days, she said—it surprised me, but I said sure, come on, and in a week or so she did. For a couple of days we saw the sights, winding our way to the top of Mount Lemmon, wandering half a day through Nogales looking at junk and tossing down tequila at Elvira's. One evening we drove out west of town and caught a sunset.

The third day she says Daddy, don't try to entertain me, just do what you always do and I'll tag along. She has a 9:07 flight back that night to Houston, which gives us all day, so I say how about the dog races? So we go for a couple of hours. I drink a few beers and lose my ten-dollar limit and we leave. This is Sunday afternoon and on the way home she acts a little miffed, not talking much. When I ask what the problem is she says something about missing church that day and feeling bad about it. I point out that it was her idea to go with me to the races, that she could have found some kind of church that would do, that Tucson is full of all kinds of churches. She says I know, I know. So we drop it.

She's restless all afternoon, like something is working on her. I figure she's anxious to get back. She flips through the

Sunday paper once and then again, like she'll come upon some answer she's looking for. I clear the table and wipe it down. I sit down with my checkbook and spread out a handful of bills. I pay bills on Sundays.

Jenny tosses the paper aside and I can tell she's watching me, but I don't look up. Finally she comes over. I'm stamping envelopes. Is this all you do? she asks. Go to the dog races and eat and pay bills? Don't you have any friends or read or go to movies?

What's wrong with that? I ask. At least I can pay my bills. And what's wrong with dog races?

I don't know what's happening, why she's angry, but an old, almost forgotten pissed-off sensation creeps back in my gut, a hell-catching sort of feeling that takes me back to times with her mother. I feel myself begin to bluster up. Yeah, Jenny, I say, sweeping my arm over the bills, giving them all a little flutter, I'm afraid that what you see is pretty much the way life is. My life, at least, is a whole lot of will the water bill be $14.88 or $16.73 and will the phone bill be under $30.00. That's why I go to the dog races. I pay these bills to keep everything the same; I pay at the races hoping to make things different.

Then she starts in on the dog races like she'd been waiting for an opening. She's going on and I'm trying to follow her. She paces the room telling me how she's figured the races out, how the mechanical rabbit's out in front and how the lead dog chases it and how all the other dogs seem only to chase the lead dog, as if there isn't a front-runner rabbit there at all. Like it's all some big joke and the dogs know, and are muzzled, not to keep them from barking or biting but to keep them from laughing at all the suckers leaning on the rail. Just one big joke, she says, with a shake of her head. I watch her soft scrambled hair move from side to side.

Then I look past her and find through the window a beam of light, all pink and purple, laced across a tiny piece of mountain way off in the distance, squeezed between a roof and a tree. Sometimes when I'm alone I sit and stare at that slice of mountain for hours. No music, the TV silent. Maybe a beer or two. Maybe more.

One minute she's staring out the window with her back to me, and then she turns and like a flash flood racing down a rocky gulch her words start flowing and they seem important, and I am quiet and still to hear what she is saying.

Do you remember when I called you from New Orleans, when I was seventeen?

I don't remember a thing, but dig around in the past trying to orient myself, where I was then, what I was doing.

You were in San Diego, she says, involved in some big project or something. I remember you sounded impatient, or important, maybe. Mama was on the extension and you made her hang up before you would talk.

Okay, I say, now it's coming back. More than twenty years ago, but yeah, it's coming back.

What was happening? she asks. Tell me what you remember.

You know, I say, that was the past, it almost seems like another life, and you were young. A long time ago.

Just tell me what you remember, she says. Jenny's pacing again and I want her to get still so I can think, but she doesn't.

Well, I say, it seems like you called. It was late I think and I could tell from the way the phone sounded you-know-who was on the extension. So I think I said, tell her to get off the line or I hang up. I may have been angry, but I had my reasons you know.

That's okay, Jenny says. I understand, but that's not the point.

Well, what the hell is the point, I say. I go to the kitchen and get a beer and stand facing her across the room.

Just tell me what happened, what you remember.

Okay, I say, this is it—in a nutshell. You were in trouble.

Pregnant, Jenny says. I was pregnant.

Okay. You were pregnant. It was some kid who worked summers on a shrimper or somewhere, a kid like you.

He was twenty.

That's still a kid in my book.

Okay, whatever you say. Then what happened?

You asked me what you should do. You and your mama had had a big fight over it and you asked me what you should do.

And what did you say?

I don't know. I can't remember exactly. I didn't want to take sides. I think you needed some money and I said I'd send it. Something like that.

Something like that, Jenny says. Yeah, it was something like that. You want to know what you said? Do you?

I drank deep from the beer. Sure. What the hell did I say?

You said, Jenny, you're young, there's plenty of time for you to have babies.

So, what else could I say? I'm not some great big daddy in the sky who knows it all. What did you want to hear?

What did I want to hear. Oh, my God, Daddy. Don't you know anything? She waits a minute and I think she will cry, but she doesn't, and when she speaks the words are all even and spaced out like studs running down a long wall. I wanted to hear you say, come to California and have your baby and it will be my grandchild and I will love you both and take care of you. That's what I wanted to hear. That's all.

I start to say that's not fair, and all the excuses, the justifications come to my mind. Your mama had custody, it was your life, what about the boy's responsibility, and on and on. But I keep quiet.

Jenny turns back to the window and her shoulders shake and then she starts sobbing, softly, quietly at first, then from deep within her comes a moan and then another one, louder and louder. From across the yard my neighbor's dogs pick up the moans and begin to howl, and soon I hear other dogs from across the street and then from all up and down the block. Finally it seems the whole world is howling.

While Jenny's packing I almost call a cab for her. I could say my ulcer is acting up or that I can't drive at night or something. But I don't.

On the way to the airport Jenny acts like nothing at all happened. She explains low impact aerobics to me, how it can give you "body confidence." She chatters on, losing me when glycogen and fats start getting together with oxygen.

When I drop her off she gives me a peck on the cheek, and I watch while she disappears up an escalator.

I drive around awhile then, glad to be alone and in a different part of the city. I circle the Night Owl Bar, checking it out, then stop back out front with the motor idling, trying to think. Finally, I pull through the drive-in window of George's Liquor next door for a pint of Old Fitz. I head north and then turn east on 22nd. The road is smooth and wide and for a few minutes I feel an old exuberance, being alone like this on an unknown road, not knowing where I'll end up.

I drive easy, letting the city thin out around me. Then up ahead I see two giant cactuses blanketed with strands of blinking white Christmas lights. I slow when I see a sign: Cactus Estates East. At the entrance the two plants flank a gleaming asphalt drive and I pull in. Loose gravel pings up under my car. A new subdivision, just getting off the ground. I know how that feels. On my right a model home glows yellow under a guard light. The subdivision is a series of cul-de-sacs that spur off the main drive, and in one I stop and turn off the engine, hoping to hear nothing, but faintly pick up the hum of I-10 in the background. I sit for a while. When the Old Fitz has smoothed the creases from the night, I decide to cruise around some more.

Back on the main drive a couple of slabs are poured, PVC sticking out of them like periscopes on a submarine. I stop and check them out. The slabs are much too close together, I think, with all this land stretching forever around. I look back west and can't see the stars for the glow from the city, but to the east the sky is filled and bright. Jenny is up there somewhere, already over New Mexico. I stare at the sky and try to make out where the brightness ends and the dullness, the murkiness, begins, try to find some absolute line where things become clear. But I can't. "Goodbye, Jenny," I say, then look around to make sure I'm alone.

The slab is rough under my feet. I talk right to it. "You're solid, good and solid," I say, "with lots of re-bar. Last a long time. What will you do?" I ask. "With all that time? With a new life, one just beginning. Is it enough to be strong? For sure you won't be running off here and there chasing God knows what all."

I laugh and take another shot of bourbon.

"But there's always the possibility of a new freeway, maybe a loop, cutting right through you. Even an earthquake. Or a fire, or even a fickle owner. Who can say?"

My voice is bolder. I hear it carry out into the dark of the desert and no longer care. "Just a crazy old man," I say, and laugh again.

I'm quiet for a few minutes and then nothing seems funny anymore. I think about dying. What nothing might be like, a bright glow, like some people near death have said, or only darkness, or maybe no sense of anything at all. For a minute I regret I can't be young again and go back and fix at least a few things. And I picture it, being young again, twenty-eight or thirty, and the whole world stretching out before me. With a new car, maybe, and good looks, and highways leading anywhere and everywhere. Seattle this time, maybe, or Portland. A boom city anywhere, somewhere new.

To the north the Santa Catalinas rise above the desert, hovering like a bank of somber clouds. I wander away from the road, by the light of the moon picking my way through the mesquite and cactus, and stop when I find a little rise that overhangs a dry wash. With my heel I make a mark in the sand, then step off twenty paces as straight as I can. Then another mark and at a right angle measure fifteen paces, then back and parallel to the first side twenty paces more and mark the sand once again. "Plenty of room for a house," I say. I could build one right here and build it right, so that it would last. And if Jenny called I would know what to do and know the right words to say.

I slip down into the wash and gather an armful of stones, as many as I can carry. Then I scramble back up the bank, searching the sand for the marks I've made, stacking stones for the corners of my house.

The Way Things Happen

THIS story begins in a Motel 6 bed in Longview, Texas. I'm leaning back against a couple of pillows I've robbed from the other bed and Jeanie's propped up beside me. My feet hurt like hell and I want my boots off, but not bad enough to move. The TV's on, but too low to hear or drown out the groan of trucks pushing by on the interstate, and we're not really watching, anyway. At least Jeanie's not. I want to but can't, not with her going on like she is.

"William?" she asks. My friends call me Billy, but from the very first, for nearly seven years, she's called me William. I like it okay. "How do you feel about chickens?"

I take a sip of my beer and don't answer right away. For one thing I never thought about it. Then I say, very slowly, "Chickens. How do I feel about chickens?" I'm saying this back aloud, you understand, but all the time I'm watching the screen, wondering how it would feel to be on a TV show like that, kissing some gorgeous woman, wondering what I would do with my hands after they glide down her body and then out of camera range. I mean this is serious. There you are kissing on cue, in front of the director and God knows who all and your hands start to move toward private places and just in time the camera zooms up close to your faces and stays there zeroed in on churning lips and tangled tongues, and I wonder, what happens with your hands. I mean what would *you* do? Just think about that a minute.

"Do chickens stink?" she asks. Then she says, "I can't quite remember. Oh, yeah, now I can. They stink a little."

"Uh-huh, a little," I say. "Not like hogs or sheep, though, I don't think."

A commercial comes on and I know why. What else can you do after a scene like that? I look over at Jeanie. She's pulled the sheet up around her, tight under her arms. She's wearing an old T-shirt of mine, her hair's still damp from the shower and pulled back in a ponytail. She's studying a chicken house probably dreamed up by Rube Goldberg's hippie grandson.

"Look at this," she says, and I look. "This one's great. It's constructed on two levels, so that the chickens live in the penthouse . . ."

"The penthouse?" I ask, but I don't laugh. None of this is funny anymore, now that Jeanie's inherited a farm and we're headed for Arkansas.

She ignores me. "The chickens live in what he calls the penthouse," and she holds up the book with her finger pointed right at the word, PENTHOUSE, written in some hippie-dippy flower-child sort of way with an arrow shooting out to the top of the drawing. "And their droppings fall into your compost pile which is here below."

She squinches up her nose when she concentrates this way. I like watching her. At thirty-seven she's still quite a woman. Her body has thickened the past few years—breasts fuller, her tummy bulges a little when she sits. But like I say, I still get a kick out of watching her, although I don't let on.

I'm not showing interest in much of anything, letting her know I'm still not sold on this farm idea. Not just the chicken house, but the whole move.

"Look at this," she says, and stabs me lightly with her elbow. "The chicken house sits in the middle of the garden and you build chicken-wire runs like this, in figure eights, like a sort of maze, and the chickens run through it and eat the bugs that fly or crawl through."

"Or hop through?" I ask.

"That wander through, smarty," she says without looking up. "Anything that moves and is smaller than a mouse, a chicken will eat." And she reaches over and pinches my bare arm, which is red from hanging out the window of the U-Haul all day.

I can't quite make out what's happening now. The gorgeous woman is talking to a rugged, handsome guy and they're both worried. Not fighting, but worried. Either the sex they had during the commercial was not quite right, or they think some other interested party will find out, or maybe it was the same old sex, the same as always, and they're asking, is that all there is? They'll probably worry all the way to the next commercial.

When we first met, Jeanie rebounding after that Frank character dropped her, she would talk about the farm for hours, like her words would bring it back for a little while. It was special to her, but she never talked about it without both laughing and crying. I always remember the crying more. Jeanie's told me, back when she was little, how she bounced all over the country, her mama always either chasing after Jeanie's daddy or hiding out from him. And always Noney's farm was a place to drop Jeanie off. Her mama would leave her "just for a few days," only until she "got things straightened out," those few days stretching into weeks or months. Jeanie can't talk about the farm without telling how she was always being left. She says her mind's all clogged up from seeing the back of her mama's car rush away in a cloud of dust.

Her mama still calls Jeanie from God knows where, always collect, says she's still trying to get things straightened out. After the calls we always have a farm talk and Jeanie ends up saying, "Noney's farm is the only piece of ground I could ever stand on without getting dizzy." And I always say, "Jeanie, a worn-out piece of ground can't hold you steady; you were hanging on to Noney, can't you see that?" But she ignores me.

Now there are two gorgeous women in a room. The first one is sitting and won't look up. She's not crying now but still looks worried. The other woman has red hair and paces up and down. I can tell there's a lot on her mind and she's letting the first gorgeous woman have a piece of it. The man is nowhere to be seen. Probably a smart move.

Now Jeanie's put the chicken-house book to one side and is studying quilt patterns in some magazine she's borrowed from her best friend, Sandy. She keeps turning the pages and saying, "I remember Noney had this one, one just like this." She creases the magazine open and then holds it out between my face and the TV. Jeanie's been saving scraps of cloth, of this and that, for months. A green garbage bag full. No polyester, she says, natural fibers only. She's begun to see herself as some earth mother type, but I don't quite buy it.

I grew up on a farm. Swore I'd never go back to that again. Not that I can't do the work; even Jeanie says I'd be a natural. That's because I'm what's called "handy." I can fix anything. You don't work in the oil patch for nearly twenty years without being handy. Roughneck, driller, toolpusher. You name it and I've done it. Made good money, too. But good times come and good times go.

* * *

I followed in the truck this morning, and Jeanie led the way in the Datsun. If it was newer it would be a Nissan, but it's a Datsun. We meant to make Texarkana but didn't, with the truck loaded down the way it is. All afternoon I watched the back of Jeanie's head, the way it moved from side to side while she drove, and I knew she was singing. Sometimes she sounds almost like Emmy Lou, just a little flatter is all. When her head stopped swaying I knew she'd stopped singing and was thinking, about what who could know? For miles it was like watching the silent TV. The truck wheels had a rhythm, a sort of tick that seemed to say over and over "what the hell you doing? where the hell you going? what the hell you doing? where the hell you going?" Damn near drove me crazy. I'd slow it down and then rev it up, hoping to find the answer at another speed. After a while I gave up and tried watching the slash pine along the road the way their tops leaned and scratched against the gray sky for miles and miles.

I've missed a lot, I guess. The gorgeous woman is walking through a garden behind a mansion. She stops and smells a rose, then we see a close-up of her face and a tear trickles down her cheek. A man comes up beside her. He's older. He says something to her. She puts her hands to her face. Then a close-up again as she fades into a commercial.

We ate at the Derrick Cafe next to the motel. Their sign outside said "We feed you, not fool you," and they did. After supper Jeanie went back to the room and I ducked into the Rio Palm Isle down the street. Can you believe naming a bar the Rio Palm Isle in Longview, Texas, three hundred miles from more than a bean pot of salt water or a palm tree? Dark, dark, dark inside. Just a little neon here and there. Once, before Jeanie, when I was somewhat of a hell-raiser, I knew a tiny thing of a woman who liked bars like that. Can't even remember her name. With her I'd have spent half the night hanging out there. But I've since learned never to trust little women. They'll lead you into dark bars and get you into big trouble. I'll drink my six-pack right here, thank you.

"William," Jeanie says. "Are you watching that?"

"A little," I say.

"Can we talk?" she asks, and I say, "Shoot, honey," pretending not to care about the TV.

"This afternoon," she says, "before we got to Lufkin, did you see how icy the clouds were, but how right above the tops of the trees, way off to the left of us, there was this line of blue stretching all the way across the sky. Did you see that?"

"Uh-huh," I say.

"Do you know what that was?" she asks.

I know a blue norther blowing in when I see it, but I figure there's more to it than that. So I wait.

"An omen." She looks at me and nods her head. "It was an omen."

"An omen," I say. "Yeah, might've been."

"It was," she says. "A good one," and starts flipping through the quilt magazine again.

Now she's crying, the gorgeous woman. Driving a new Corvette and crying. They set it all up this way. Sometimes I don't even listen to the TV stories; I just try to figure the way they've set it all up. I tried to explain it to Jeanie, but she said they're all just stories, anyway. Some you like and some you don't like and that's all there is to it. That's what she said. I know better, but what's the point in arguing?

Before we left, Jeanie went next door to Sandy's and gave her our new address, some rural route and box that I don't even know yet. She said, "Sandy, now don't you let a soul have this except for Amy." That's Jeanie's daughter. Amy. Sixteen going on twenty-five and in California the last we heard. Said she was going to live with her daddy. Well, good luck was all I said to that, but it hurt Jeanie real bad. Jeanie cried and carried on for days about always being left, always being alone. She kept moaning "alone again, alone again, alone again," over and over. I was with her the whole time, but if she couldn't see that, I figured it wasn't my place to tell her.

I did try to talk to her, to let her know I understood, that being alone's no big news to me. I said Jeanie, being alone's old hat for me. You work graveyard in the tower of a derrick miles out in the Gulf of Mexico and you know all about it. I mean, there's the driller and a half-dozen roughnecks down below on the deck, but you're eighty feet above them swinging drill pipe into place and the lights are so bright up there you're blinded to everything outside the circle they make and the rig's vibrating so that you can hardly piss in the coffee can you keep up there, and noise, well, all there is is noise. And you can't see it, but you know how deep and dark the water is for miles around. But it's funny, with all that dark and shaking and noise, how after seven or eight hours, the loud is so loud that it becomes quiet to you, where you don't even hear it, like you're in a capsule of some kind, sealed off alone from the rest of the world.

She said William, I don't think you really understand at all.

Well, shit on you, too, I thought at the time, but didn't say it.

I first met Jeanie seven years ago and right off the bat she tells me about having Amy, and I say to myself, uh-oh, that's trouble. Later, after Amy skipped off out west, I told Jeanie all about it, how Amy is a jinx of a name. Jeanie, I said, the youngest widow I ever knew was Amy B. Aaron and we went to Kirbyville High School together. I never knew what the B. stood for, but she dated Lee Forester all through school. Lee was a little older and drove a dump truck hauling gravel or brush or whatever he could to make a living. Before they got married Lee and Amy used to go to the drive-in every Saturday night and old Lee would back that big sucker of a truck next to a speaker in the back row. Then he'd tilt the bed just a little and they'd set up their lawn chairs, you know those plastic-web folding kind, in the back, and they'd take it all in. Holding hands. They weren't married more than a couple of months when Lee let that truck roll back and crush him against a loading dock. Amy B. Aaron, the youngest widow I ever knew. Now that's being left alone.

You know what Jeanie said to that? She said, "William, do you know that every time I try to tell you about a problem, before I've even gotten it out, I see you going off somewhere in your head, fishing up some crazy sort of story. All I want is for you to listen. Can't you ever just listen?"

"I guess not," is all I said.

"Sweetheart," I say and reach over to take her hand, but she's writing down something she's found in the chicken-house book, so I squeeze her leg through the covers. "I've been thinking about the farm—are you listening?"

"Uh-huh," she says without looking up.

"How about this for an idea," I say, " purely from a business standpoint, you understand." She still doesn't look up, so I say, "Jeanie, this is important."

"Okay," she says, and folds the book closed, marking her place with a finger.

"Now listen all the way through before you say a word. Will you?"

"I promise," she says, but holds up her free hand and shows me her crossed fingers and laughs.

"This is serious, sweetheart," I say, and she locks her lips with a twist of her fingers and throws away the key.

"Now this is just an idea, you understand," I say again.

"William, what is it? Just say what it is."

"Just hold on, I'm getting there. Now I've been doing some reading, some reading and some thinking and I figure this. One, the oil business is on the way back. I mean, in six months, six months at the latest, oil rigs'll be thick as grasshoppers all over South Texas and a man could work seven days a week if he wanted to."

Jeanie lays the book down between us and folds her arms, pulling them up tight.

"Given that, why would a man want to leave? It'd be like walking away from a gold mine."

"Fool's gold, if you ask me," Jeanie says. "And we've already walked away."

"Uh-uh. No talking, you promised," I say, then go on. "Now the problem, we both know, is the six months. The house is gone, but we didn't have much in it, and rent is cheap."

"House payments were cheap."

"We got behind's the problem," I say. "I just now came up with the answer."

"Was it on the TV?" she asks, with a toss of her head, but I ignore it.

"It's so simple," I say. "We sell the farm, pay off our bills, have a nice fat CD in the bank. Then we rent a little place temporarily and wait it out."

Jeanie jumps out of bed, and starts pacing. I can see the lace of her panties under her shirt as she strides back and forth across the room.

"It's only an idea," I say. "I'll be lost on a farm in Arkansas. You know that."

"Can I talk now, William. Can I talk?" she says, her voice bouncing around the room. She stops pacing, both hands on her hips, and looks at me like I'm a candidate for road-kill chili. "What about me, William? What about me? You want me to put in nine more years out at the Ford plant? Is that what you want from me?" She starts pacing again and I just watch.

"The farm was Noney's and now it's mine—not ours, mine, you understand? It's not just a piece of land holding the earth together. Don't you even care about the way I feel?"

"Well, hell," I say. "What about me, too. Going God-knows-where to some place I've never been, a place you can hardly remember. Everything I own in a goddamn U-Haul truck, following some woman to Arkansas. Sometimes I feel like a trained poodle instead of a man."

"I'm not 'some woman,'" she says, "at least I hope not." She laughs a shallow laugh. "And you may be some kind of a dog, William, but you're no poodle."

Then she softens, sits beside me on the edge of the bed. "William, you're my husband and the only man I ever really truly loved, but that farm may be the only thing I can count on never to go away, never to disappear."

"Now, wait just a minute," I say, but she's not finished.

"What can *you* count on, William? Where's that job that looked so good a year ago? What happened to that little nest egg we had? We drove away from a house I thought would always be ours just this morning."

"Okay, okay," I say. "Just forget it." But there's no stopping her now.

"And what about me?" she asks. "What about you? Are we both all that reliable? I mean, we've had our times, re-member?" She stops a minute to catch her breath. "When you get down to it all you have is you, and all I have is—myself and the farm."

"I don't buy that," I say. "No way I'll buy that." But right now I don't know what else to buy, so I concentrate hard on the screen, wishing my world was in a little box like that. Tonight I'd turn it off for a while.

Jeanie crawls back under the covers, way over on her side of the bed, shivering just a little. She picks up her book but just hugs it and stares hard at the TV, too.

In a couple of minutes she sticks one foot out from under the sheet and starts flaking the red off the nail of her big toe. Then she says, "You know I didn't mean to snap at you, don't you, sweetheart? But that farm is my dream, and you know how dreams are."

I reach over and pat her on the leg, my eyes still on the TV. We're getting to the good part. But Jeanie's still not farmed out.

"The flowers Noney had, you should have seen them. And the garden. Green beans and new potatoes every day. Dirt, nice clean dirt under your fingernails. Iced tea every evening on the porch swing. But you'll see."

"William," she says again, her voice high and soft, "did I ever tell you about when I was little, maybe three or four, and I used to help Noney gather eggs?"

"Uh-huh. You did."

"I remember those red hens," she says. "God, they looked big as eagles to me, squawking and fluttering when Noney shooed them off their nests. Then she'd hold me up so I could reach into those deep dark nests. We'd take those eggs inside. Oh, they were huge and brown. We'd draw water into one of her blue splattered pans and wipe all the eggs clean. Noney would let me put them in rows in a cardboard holder, you know the kind, one at a time until it was all filled up."

I've heard this all before, but I don't stop her. Usually she starts up on the eggs and chickens and the farm on Sundays, after we've made love and gone to Denny's for breakfast and the Oilers are playing some big game, and it's my day off. She'd be on the sofa with me, all quiet, sewing something or flipping through one of her magazines and out of the blue she'd start up about the farm. She could go on about chickens and eggs forever.

"William," she says, snuggling up against me, "I had secrets then. Not like the ones I had later, but good, clean secrets. Places to hide, behind the old cistern or in a rotted-out stump. And did I tell you," she asks and laughs out loud, "how all one afternoon I slid down the shed roof and ripped my pants on the tin and how, every time it happened, I would run in the house and change because Noney had told me never to be seen going around looking raggedy. I ruined every pair of pants I had."

From the corner of my eye I see her shake her head and get real still for a minute like she's gone off somewhere dreamy, and then she starts flipping through the quilts again, humming quietly to herself.

"I don't think I can sleep," Jeanie says. The quilt magazine is open and face down across her tummy and I watch it move up and down as she talks. She reaches out her hand and pats my arm. "Aren't you excited, honey?" she asks. Now *she's* staring at the TV. It's another commercial. "Just think," she says, "tomorrow night at this time we'll be in our own house on our own farm." Then she squeezes my hand and lets it go. "Do you think we'll always be there?" she asks. "I mean, will we be happy and settled and will the farm be home? I mean really home?"

I don't answer for a minute and we both stare at the screen. Then I say, "You sure there's a tractor there? No way this'll work without a tractor." She just nods.

The first gorgeous woman is in her Corvette again. Driving too fast. We flash back to the other gorgeous woman. She's in some sort of a dressing gown. The man is with her. The room darkens. I know what's going to happen. Then the Corvette is on a winding mountain road with lots of hairpin curves. Now back to the couple. They're moving right along. Desperate, heavy breathing. We get a close-up of their faces. Where are their hands, I wonder. Now the Corvette is going into a spin. A lot of smoke and next thing you know it's crumpled into a tree. I know how they do that. If you're handy with cameras and splicing film you can make anything happen.

I say, Jeanie, honey, you know how they do that? Well, let me tell you how it works. First you've got to be handy, and then you take two or maybe three different Corvettes and a bunch of cameras everywhere and maybe even a dummy or two. I look over, but she's already asleep.

I flip off the lamp by the bed and stare at the screen, but everything's different, a whole new set of characters talking, moving around in some newspaper office like they've been there forever. Now you can catch up on a story like this in a hurry if you know how it all works, and I do. But it's late and I don't care.

I move to the window and pull the curtain to one side, holding it, and look out into the night. The silver of the U-Haul glows in the amber lights. So much stuff locked in there; and I try to remember what it is, and why I would ever have bought it, and if I still want whatever it is anyway. I watch as a car accelerates up the ramp and onto the interstate, losing itself on the empty highway, hurrying on to someplace else in a deliberate sort of way. A place that maybe I could go.

I let the curtain fall back, and as it brushes my face, the smell of the motel closes in, a musty, smoky, Lysol smell, one that brings back other times, before Jeanie. And then the room itself closes in, small and tight as a chicken coop at midnight. And I feel again all those nights on the road, living in motels, living with that smell. And so many days alone in between.

I sink back down on the bed, watching how the light from the TV flashes across Jeanie's face, how she seems so fragile in her sleep.

Now I can't fortune-tell. This is tonight, and tomorrow's tomorrow, but you want to know how it'll be and I'll tell you. It'll go like this. We'll drive up to Noney's farmhouse, the U-Haul following the dust of the Datsun. I can see it just like a movie. We stop and sit for a minute while the wind sucks the dust away. I watch from the truck while Jeanie walks through the front gate and stops. The house is gray as the sky. The front porch droops, and a porch swing hangs on end, dangling from one rusty chain. The yard is bare except for some shrubs that reach wild up past the windows. Jeanie turns and looks at me and tries a smile, but it doesn't take. Then she turns back and I see her shoulders sag, and she wags her head side to side like she's singing, but I know she's not.

I want to talk to Jeanie, tell her how things end up in certain ways, how things aren't always the way they look, don't stay the way you remember. I want to wake her, to say Jeanie, Jeanie, you have to understand. Let me explain, let me tell you the way things happen.

Disappearing

LELAND called me at four this morning. No hello, no preliminaries. "Hey, Willy," he said, "when even your wet dreams are unhappy, it's time for a change. Let's take a ride deep into Mexico and talk about women."

I'm on my own a couple of weeks while Patty's in Tulsa visiting her folks. I'm supposed to be looking for a job, but Leland's not just some beer drinking buddy, he's my darts partner. So when he called I said what the hell, let's go.

Leland's a smart guy, a lawyer. Big Dallas law firms drop off bundles of title company abstracts at his house and Leland works up title opinions and modems them back downtown. He's a genius at land titles, everyone says, and is fast. Sometimes we're at the Quiet Man, been playing 301 for a couple of hours, it'll be eleven at night and Leland will pop his darts back in their case. "Time to go to work," he'll say, and by morning will have ghosted a five-hundred-dollar title opinion. Leland's good. Damn near a genius—but not your typical Dallas lawyer.

Why he targeted me for a darts partner is hard to guess. When you're in a class by yourself, maybe it doesn't matter who you're with. I've seen him make 301 in twelve darts, not a world record by a long shot but good enough to draw a crowd at the Quiet Man.

We took my Toyota, a cooler in the back, and slipped quickly south through the dark Dallas morning hoping to make the border at Laredo by afternoon. From there we planned to wander a couple of hundred miles further southwest across the Chihuahuan desert to Saltillo. On the way down we pit-stopped at a Shamrock for gas and Honey Buns and coffee and then Leland fell into a deep sleep while I maneuvered in and out of Austin's midmorning brashness and down through San Antonio to where the country flattens into a scattering of mesquite.

Leland wakes up talking about dreams. While he's going on he waves his arms, jabbing dents in the softness of the dashboard. A dent for every point he makes. Leland is a large man: large hands, a big bony frame and a beard that bushes out wild, sometimes in this and sometimes in that direction. In Dallas he is a man out of place, but get him headed towards Mexico and he fits right in the way only a crazy gringo can.

"Bad dreams," Leland says, "are caused by a stutter in the magnetic field, a result of tectonic slipping and sliding. In California this causes earthquakes, but the stress in the midlands, in constipated places such as Dallas, is less obvious but just as wrenching. The result is bad dreams. Bad, bad dreams."

I don't say so but Leland only has bad dreams after a woman leaves him. I know that and he knows I know that. Leland's called other mornings at one and two and three o'clock—a different woman each time, a trip to Mexico in the works. I could never go before. Or that's not exactly right. I never could bring myself to tell Patty that I was running off to Mexico with Leland. She calls him "that wild man." She says that at thirty-two I'm too old for that anyway. Only horny college kids run off to Mexico. She doesn't quite understand. First of all, after a man reaches thirty or so, sex has only an incidental relationship to horniness; and second, running off to Mexico is not entirely irresponsible, but may have something to do with lessening that trail of regret that can't help but accumulate behind you as you go. We've been married for eight years now, and with no offspring in sight the tie that binds seems to have gotten a little frazzled as of late. But maybe that's just me. Disappointment showed on neither of our faces, however, when Patty's trip to Tulsa came up.

Anyway, the timing seemed right. Leland called and Mexico lay fat and sassy to the south.

We cross the border midafternoon, leaving all sorts of garbage behind. I had promised Patty that I'd look for a job while she's gone, and that begins to eat on me, but Leland smooths it away. "You have a job," he says. "You're a teacher, an able-bodied, ass-kicking, mind-stretching teacher of the first class. The schools close for the summer and you think it's your fault? And anyway," he adds, "you didn't say where you'd look for a job, and the way things stink in Texas, Mexico might be a better bet." Leland's advice is good when it's what you want to hear.

In the *mercado* Leland first thing spots a sign that says "No Problem Taco." While we eat I'm praying this is no gringo joke. Leland finds *limóns*, mottled yellow-green, not much bigger than marbles, and all the Tecate we can carry. Pemex cheerily knocks whenever I floorboard the car. Leland tells me about the *limóns*, the way the big fruit growers have conspired so that you'll never find these little jewels in a Safeway. He cuts a dozen into halves and lines them up on the dashboard where we watch them rock and roll.

I wish I could have videotaped Leland in the market. Somehow south of the border he changes, the lawyer tension leaves his face and he resurrects his sense of humor. He pulls his straw hat down low. Then he lifts the hat and points to his thinning hair. "Can't fry this," he says, "that's where I store my brains." He's dressed all in white with a necklace of lapis, blue as the Caribbean, hanging among the hairs on his chest. Limes are a few pesos a dozen, maybe a nickel or dime in U.S. dollars, but Leland goes from stall to stall. "*Cuánto cuesta?* How much?" he asks. Then "Ooh, *muy caro*, too much," he says, like he's been stabbed with the answer, and he moves on to the next vendor. He buys six dozen limes. Says we'll smuggle the leftovers back across the border on Sunday. Life's an adventure, he tells me. Life for Leland is one big attempt to beat the system, I think.

When we're out of Laredo a few miles and through the *inspección federal*, Leland opens a couple of Tecates and eases into his story, like this is the time he's been waiting for. Last night, he tells me, it was Carol Ann. She's hung around the Quiet Man before, but for the past couple of months I could tell she and Leland had something going. One thing, he lost his famous 301 concentration and we had to buy beers more nights than I like to remember. You can tell when something's in the air, when Leland's sniffing and barking, no longer content to howl at the moon.

By the time we hit Sabinas Hidalgo the whole story is out. I drive, one eye on the road ahead, passing families huddled in the back of shimmy-assed pickups, slowing for the speed bumps that mark the bus stops every few miles, the other eye alert to buses and trucks that roar up behind and blat-blat-blat as they slow right on my bumper before blasting around, lights flashing. Mexican kamikazes, Leland says.

Carol Ann, it turns out, was not all that she appeared to be. She left Leland's last night about midnight, as he tells it, after a couple of White Russians and a joint to top off a strenuous hour or so thrashing around on his waterbed.

Carol Ann is a dancer, has even been in a production or two at the Dallas Theater Center and, although she's only twenty-seven, has choreographed some punk storefront version of *Salome* that had the Dallas vice squad in attendance. She's on the edge, and Leland fell for her hard. A soul mate of sorts, I suppose, even with the difference in their ages.

"Well," Leland says, "she left and I was out like that, I mean as my daddy would say, plumb tuckered out. But sometime between then and two o'clock here comes this dream. There's Carol Ann, dancing with these flimsy veils swishing this way and that. She's not really dancing, though, not on the floor anyway. She's sort of floating around. We're in a strange room, and I'm naked on my waterbed. She dances back and forth across the bed, sexy as hell, teasing me. I can still feel the waterbed rocking and swishing, matching the rhythm of the music. I get this hard-on that won't wait, but when I try to get her to stop swirling and twirling she leaves the room. In a minute she comes back leading this young hunk of a guy by the hand and I know he's her lover. Well, they start to get it on right there in front of me, and I'm twisting and turning, trying to grab her, to stop them, but I'm tangled in the sheets so all I can do is watch her with this other guy."

He stops then for a minute. "You want another Tecate, Willy?" he asks and I nod.

"So that's your unhappy wet dream?" I ask.

"Let me tell you what else," he says. "I wake up then all agitated. It's two in the morning and I'm craving something sweet, thinking that will soothe the savage beast. So I go to the kitchen and stick my head in the refrigerator, but everything that should be hard is soft and everything that should be soft is hard. So I'm standing there wondering if I could get Dunkin' Donuts to deliver when the phone rings."

Leland pops another Tecate and I can see that the empties are winning. He squeezes a couple of lime halves in the can and tosses them out the window. "Biodegradable," he says, looking straight ahead. He's quiet a minute.

I gaze out across the desert and find one little patch of agave plants, about a dozen rows. A man slowly hoes around one of the plants and I wonder what he's thinking about—the tequila those plants will make, or some woman, or a Kubota tractor he once saw in Monterrey. Or maybe he's dreaming of breaking that hoe across his knee and walking away from what has to be a miserly and narrow life. Does he ever get that far along, I wonder? Far enough past the margins of his life, one of tortillas and beans and a rotten tooth that needs to come out and too many kids? Does the need to run away, or better, to run *to* something, some sort of adventure, only click in after you're at the equivalent level of a spoiled American? Probably, sadly so.

Leland's gone off somewhere. "Okay," I say. "It's two in the morning, you've got a severe case of the munchies, and the phone rings."

He snaps back with me. "It's Carol Ann," he says, and I'm not surprised one bit. "She got back to her apartment and skinny-ass Roland, you know, the *jefe* from the Theater Center, had a message on her machine to call. Seems they had a cancellation and would give Carol Ann three dead days in August to stage her *Salome*, providing she would keep it on the inside edge of Dallas clean. A big break for her."

"Hey," I say, "no way that's bad news, is it?"

Leland shrugs and when he starts to talk his voice takes on a detached sort of lawyer distance, like it's not him talking at all. "So what does one do upon receiving glad tidings? This one, as it turns out, pops a cork of the best at hand, a sickly sweet white zin if I were guessing, and proceeds to get loaded while calling her ragtag dance troupe for an impromptu celebration. Problem is, at that hour only flat-bellied Barry what's-his-name shows up, with his flute and a bottle of pink bubbly. Well," Leland says, and stops long

enough to catch a deep breath. "Isn't this disgustingly predictable? Which came first? Barry's version of Ravel's *Bolero*
or Carol Ann breaking out the seven veils, or, later, the rit-
ualistic placing of the empties in the glass-to-be-recycled
pail. And all the time it's happening I'm twisted up in my
sheets dreaming it. Shit." Leland shakes his head in disgust
and falls back on the lawyer in him. "What are the reasons
for a woman to have sex anyway? When desire meets op-
portunity? When some esoteric chemical congruence oc-
curs? Is it her way of running off to the Mexico of her
mind?"

"Why'd she call?" I ask. "Some way to get back at you for
something?"

"Who knows?" he says. "She tried to turn it around, make
it all my fault. Said something like 'you're always such a
lawyer' when I tried to reason with her. But I figure it was
plain old guilt, probably. Drunken confession often seems
to be the right fix for a tarnished soul. And it may have been
fine for Carol Ann's soul, but let me tell you, Willy, it wasn't
worth a shit for mine."

"To hell with women," I say, for Leland or for me I'm not
sure. "To hell with all the damn women of the world."

We drink to that and we're quiet then for a long time.

"To disappear is not all that easy," Leland says. He's been
talking a while about options. What a man can do when his
life turns sour.

We're in Saltillo at the Club 45, standing at the bar. Leland finally looks comfortable, like he's been here a hundred
nights before. He nurses a Dos Equis lager from a green
longneck. He's now settled into maintenance drinking, as he
calls it, just enough to keep an edge. He has one Red Wing
boot propped on the rail. He rolls the sleeves of his shirt up
halfway, "keeps your elbows from getting raw," he says. We
started out at the hotel lounge, the Arizpe Sainz, but after
one tequila solo Leland said we needed to go to a bar, a real

one where you could get away from all the gringos. A place where you could drink and talk and piss in Mexican.

I look around. The Club 45 is just right—dark, full of strange talk, half-full of locals. Not a Ladies Bar, men only. Patty wouldn't like that a damn bit, but she wouldn't stick her toe in a place like this anyway, so who cares? A couple of quick and lean boxers flash around the TV screen at one end of the bar. That and the glow from a quartet of beer signs provide the only light. No gringos here, for sure. Leland and I see ourselves in some other category, never quite defined, but certainly not as tourists. We're wrestling with the serious issues of life.

"No," Leland says again, "to flat-ass disappear is not all that easy. I mean to really disappear, to vanish from whatever job you've got. To kiss off your family and girlfriends, to burn your social security number, give up your credit cards, your drinking buddies, to give up even your ego that keeps reminding you you're not just a bag of bones with a built-in timer that could buzz at any moment, but have a degree or two and were told in the second grade that you should be governor someday, and maybe also once a professor said you were brilliant—something you accidentally or deliberately let slip in drunken bar-talk moments. All that stuff that props you up. Let it go and disappear. Just like that. Poof."

I'd wondered about that myself, why more people don't disappear. I've known of a half-dozen people who've committed suicide, their lives so snarled that the entanglements got beyond untangling. Why didn't they just clean the slate, walk away, become a short order cook in Albuquerque or Phoenix? Would that be so much harder on whoever they left behind? A second (or a third or exponentially on) chance? A fresh start? Without regret. That's the hard part—without regret. Or at least without that old bugaboo guilt.

But Leland doesn't need to hear this. "Man," I say, "if I

had it made like you, disappearing's the last thing I'd do. Forget Carol Ann. A man like you deserves more from a woman than just being young and half-crazy. Somewhere out there in the future, maybe next week, maybe even back at the hotel there's a woman for you that's better."

"Willy, I'm not getting any younger, you know," he says, and I can tell he's sinking fast.

A fellow edges up next to us, a stringy little Mexican with a grin. "You know deep dish pizza?" he asks Leland. "For two years I live in Chicago and make deep dish pizza. Pepperoni, mozzarella, green peppers, black olives, mushrooms." He stops a minute to catch his breath and think. "Anchovies. You no like anchovies? We cut anchovies. Much things to make pizza. Eulalio Sanchez learn them all. Learn good English, too."

"Damn good English," Leland says and steps back a bit to check Eulalio out, and something special gleams in his eyes. "You have deep dish pizza for me?" he asks.

"My friend, we go to Chicago, Eulalio make for you much pizza. No pay for you. But, no. In Saltillo is no pizza. Many good things in this city, but no deep dish pizza."

Leland laughs then, the first time all day. We introduce ourselves and Leland buys Eulalio a beer and the bartender brings us a plate of *antojitos* to munch on, shredded chicken and jalapenos wrapped in tortillas. Leland and Eulalio get in a big discussion about Chicago, where Leland has spent some time. And Eulalio goes into excruciating detail describing how he got there and exactly where the pizza place is and who the big pizza boss is and what kind of car he drives—I catch Leland helping Eulalio say "Oldsmobile." Eulalio repeats it a half-dozen times, having a rough time with the first syllable, but finally they're both satisfied and move on.

I'm beginning to fade a little, not drunk at all with the beers spread out over the whole day, but I feel a deep down in the bone weariness that won't go away. Maybe all that talk about women and being unhappy and disappearing, starting over, has made me uneasy. There in that dark bar I try to back away from myself, to see where I've come to now. With Patty, who all of a sudden I feel I don't know at all, and with myself, who in this smelly Mexican bar seems to be just as much a stranger. I shake the feeling off. I'm here because I choose to be here, by God, just an ordinary man with bar-red elbows and a bad need to piss.

When I come back from the *baño* a man has taken my place at the bar. Both he and Eulalio are leaning across in front of Leland, listening and nodding. By now Leland's really revved up and onto the government, how they're the same in Mexico and in the States, "everywhere the government is made up of dirty rascals," he says. Then he stops a minute, trying to find if he's stored "dirty rascals" anywhere in the Mexican part of his brain. The best he can come up with is *bandidos*, which Eulalio and his friend affirm with solemn shakes of their heads and the clink of beer bottles.

I tell Leland I'll be back, and he just nods. Eulalio's friend extends his hand. It's cool and wet from the bottle of beer. He tells me that he is Alfredo and that he has a taxi, a good taxi, that will take me somewhere if I wish. "Very cheap," he says. I say *gracias* no, and find my way out into the Saltillo streets where it is dark.

I walk for a while. The streets have come back to life for the night. I stop by a cafe window and stare at *cabrito* stretched and roasting over chunks of orange coals. The goats are small and look strangely naked, exposed there in the window, and I have a little ache somewhere down deep for them, or for something. A feeling that I ignore. The meat is tender and juicy, packed into a warm tortilla with chopped radishes and onions and cilantro. I walk and eat and I wipe the drippings that slide down my chin with the sleeve of my shirt and it feels good.

I stop by the hotel and sneak a look in the dark bar. A

couple of tables of tourists are cussing the Astros. The bartender leans against the bar, glassy eyes fixed on the TV. At the desk I ask if there are any messages, and the clerk apologetically shrugs. No messages, *señor*. You never know, I think. Sometimes messages come in the strangest ways. I feel I could use one now.

When I get back the Club 45 is packed and dark and loud. Not with the loudness of an American bar, all boisterous and show-offy, but simply with talk, everyone talking at once. The men seem earnest, as if they have something to say and mean it.

I don't see Leland, but Alfredo is still hunched over the bar and I slide in next to him.

"Oh, *Señor* Willy," he says, as if we are old pals. "You go for a long time. Looking for girls maybe?"

My eyes have adjusted to the gloom and I look around for Leland, figure he's found someone else to try his Tex-Mex brand of talking on.

"*Señor* Leland is not here," Alfredo says with a puzzled shrug. "He left with my friend Eulalio. But he said, 'Alfredo, you must wait here for my *amigo* Willy and give this to him.' He tried to give me money," he says proudly, "but I said no."

Alfredo hands me a carefully peeled Dos Equis label, folded once. Inside, big and bold, scrawled diagonally across is one word—ADIOS. "Well, I'll be damned," I say to a puzzled Alfredo, "the son-of-a-gun has disappeared. *Es todo?*" I ask. "That is all?" Alfredo nods his head and turns back to his beer.

I tell myself that this is some kind of a joke, that Leland's back in a corner of the bar watching me try to figure this out. I stay there next to Alfredo and watch a dubbed version of "Bonanza." Every time the bar door swings open I cut my eyes around, thinking it will be Leland, but after a while I give up and wobble back to the hotel. *Mañana*, I tell myself as I collapse into bed. My last thought before sleep is that

Eulalio must have taken Leland to find a woman. He'll come dragging his sorry ass in later.

The next morning I have *huevos a la Mexicana* alone in the courtyard, and find myself getting worried about Leland. What if it was a setup and Eulalio and some pals rolled him. He has a wad of bills that he'd better not let get away. The hotel charge is his. That was our deal and Leland better not screw that up or he'll have hell to pay.

I wander the streets. Saturday morning is bright, the sun gleams off the barren mountains to the north, shopkeepers sweep the sidewalks and talk. Midmorning I stop for sweet dark coffee and decide to forget about Leland. If he doesn't show by tomorrow morning I'll just head on back. The room is in his name. Let the Arizpe Sainz worry about where Leland's gone. I say this, but find myself feeling pissed just the same. In a small shop I find a silver bracelet for Patty. I'll save it for her birthday, or just give it to her if I tell her about coming here.

Back at the hotel the clerk stops me. There is no message, but something I should know. The room has been paid through that night. When I ask about it he just shrugs.

So at least Leland's alive, I figure, and around somewhere, so I stop worrying and decide to siesta with the rest of Saltillo. Afterwards, I hang around the hotel lobby a couple of hours watching the street. When I finally step out it is just dark. Alfredo is sitting on the hood of his taxi outside the hotel and greets me like a brother. I ask if he has seen Leland or Eulalio and he says no, but if I like he will see what he can do. He has many friends, he says. He waits then and is quiet until I figure this out. Finally I catch on and hand him a five dollar bill, cussing Leland under my breath. But I play out my part of the ritual. "To find him you will need gas," I say. He protests but only for a moment, then takes the five. As he drives off I tell him I'll be either at the hotel or the Club 45. "No problem," he says. "No problem."

* * *

It's nine o'clock on a Saturday night and the Club 45 has fallen silent. This is serious. James Bond is putting the make on Pussy Galore in Spanish. When they fade under the silk sheets, the room lets out a sigh of relief and envy, followed by some uneasy laughs and joking, then settles back into its smooth rhythm. I find it hard to blend in like Leland does. He finds the Mexican men easy to be with in a way that I can't. It's funny, but back at the Quiet Man it's just the opposite. I can bullshit with the best of them while Leland isolates himself in a corner and drinks when he's not tossing darts. A stranger in his own land, I guess.

I feel a light nudge at my elbow. It's Alfredo. "Come with me," he says.

I ask if he's found Leland, but he says again, "Come with me," and leads me to his taxi. Saltillo is a hilly town, and the taxi strains in first gear as we climb out west to its edge. Then Alfredo turns down a side street and cruises slowly, easing side to side to miss the potholes. I begin to worry, wonder if this whole thing is some kind of rip-off. I ride with my hand on the door handle, ready to bolt if I sense trouble.

When we turn a corner I see a house lit up on the right. It glows like Christmas, with hundreds of tiny red lights strung across the front, sparkling in the night. The house and the adobe wall and the two cars parked in front are pink in the glare. "My friend is here?" I ask. Alfredo has a big grin and nods. "I tell you. No big problem for Alfredo."

I can't believe it. A whorehouse. That son-of-a-gun has fallen in love with a whore. Well, that figures.

The front gate is open and I step inside, checking the place out. The house is lit up and guitar music floats out through the yard over the soft laugh of a woman. Through a window I see several tables, then to my surprise, three teenage girls and a boy at one, and at another a couple with a baby. They all appear to be eating. This is no whorehouse. Then I see Leland, standing behind the counter gesturing to a woman who covers her mouth with a shawl when she laughs. His straw hat is shoved back high on his head and he's wrapped in a white apron. Then from behind him Eulalio hurries in from the back carrying a pizza on what looks like a flattened shovel. When I move to the door I notice a sign that smells of fresh paint.

DOS AMIGOS

DEEP DISH PIZZA

I slip in and Leland looks up from making change just like he's been expecting me. I start to ask what the hell he thinks he's doing disappearing like this, scaring the devil out of me, but when I see his face all serious and content at once, I don't.

"One slice?" he asks, "and a beer?"

"No anchovies," I say, and he relays the order to Eulalio. "Be just a couple of minutes," he says. I reach for my billfold but Leland stops me, hands me the beer. "No problem," he says with a grin.

I nod. "No problem, *amigo.*"

I sit outside on the porch and eat. Inside Leland's punching down a huge mound of dough through a blizzard of flour. He seems to rise as he works, growing until he almost fills the room. For a minute I wonder if Leland and Eulalio could use a partner, and I try to picture myself there, but it doesn't quite work.

When I finish the pizza I start to go back inside, but instead wave through the window. Leland doesn't see me.

Alfredo comes up beside me. "I take you somewhere now?" he asks. "Taxi very cheap. Maybe to the hotel?"

"Home," I say. "Just take me home."

Can You Get
There from Here?

Royce called her "darlin'" before the trouble and "honey" afterwards. He never, ever called her Irene.

"Darlin'," Royce said, "you turn forty and you're getting the longest Cadillac they make." He looked up at the ceiling, and then like he'd read some magic words in the cracking paint. "Yeah, a Coupe de Ville, darlin', one the color of a rose."

Irene gave him one of her you're-such-a-tease looks and laughed, but she could tell he meant it and she wanted to believe him bad, although she thought Cadillacs much too long to be practical and knew that her friend Reba would think her uppity and would find some way to let her know. But Carolee would love it, being eleven and already warting Irene to let her drive.

By that summer of the trouble Royce had revved himself up to latch on to the ripples of a boom that spread across oil patch country and found its way into that little part of northeast Texas where they lived. Those times were good for Texas, and good for any man who had the quickness and daring to play the oil game with its startling gyrations. Those times were good for Irene, too, for with Royce wheeling and dealing, her life was as light as spring air and she danced through most of her days.

And some nights, too. In those early years Irene and Royce waltzed through the house, circling the oak table, dodging the marble top buffet that had been Irene's mama's. Willie Nelson spilled his brand of melancholy through the rooms, the curtains hugged the windows tight. While Irene spun, her eyes found as a balance point the door to the bedroom where she hoped Carolee slept and wouldn't wake.

Back in the living room Royce held Irene close and they moved in tighter and tighter circles. He wore only his blue-striped pajama bottoms. Her gown's ribbon of a shoulder strap slid off her shoulder and she let it be. On the mantle a straw-covered bottle held a candle that flickered and dripped. The record gave a scrape and a sigh at the end and they collapsed laughing on the sofa.

And in those moments of softness and flickering half-light, the world and all its weight burst apart and fell from Irene.

Afterwards, Irene would watch Royce. He had his moments of ritual, the deliberate way he tapped a pack of Camels, the way he drew a cigarette from its sheath with his lips, not talking, concentrating every ounce of energy, the way he tossed his head with the first puff, his eyes heavy-lidded against the smoke. He was a handsome enough man and Irene's equivalent on that mysterious scale that most of the time accurately pairs couples together. But whereas Irene's delicacy of limb and pale skin gave her an air of paperlike fragility, Royce had a startling big-boned rough-and-readiness that caught everyone's attention.

But even though he was a man of large frame and long limbs his hands were delicate, refined, like he might have somehow taken a wrong turn back up the road that hid from him his true calling as a pianist or maybe a surgeon.

As it was, from what Irene knew, his road had been more washboard gravel than blacktop and only now with life full and swelling up around did he seem to have found an ease he had earlier missed.

Royce disclosed only enough about his past, and then with what Irene later saw as an unnatural reticence, for her to reach a point of comfort with him. A place where she could say, Irene, accept this man for what he is; and she did. For he seemed to possess whatever it might take to fill out her life.

There was a problem, as it turned out. But the problem wasn't Royce's brains or looks or charm or even drive, for he prided himself, and rightly so, on possessing a generous amount of each. Irene's best friend and every-Thursday-morning hairdresser Reba Bell had said Royce could "charm the pelt off a possum." That was before he had become a permanent and legal part of Irene's life, and came from Reba, Irene thought, half as cautionary advice and half as un-customarily petty envy. Reba had been second chair at Mi-Lady's Beauty Salon for over twelve years and may have been stuck coiffure-wise in the fifties, but she had no peer in dispensing wisdom, especially when it came to men. Irene had learned to ignore Reba's "pig in a poke" sorts of phrases, but sat up and took notice when she came out with the "charm the pelt off a possum" ones. Reba came up with that kind only at important moments, and Irene paid attention.

As Irene saw it, the problem behind the trouble may have sprung from Royce's reach, the way he could unfold those freckled arms and stretch them, it seemed like forever, grasping for, then latching onto more than he could hold, which is all right if you can do it properly and know when to gracefully pull back, when to let go. But Royce's grasp was door-slam tight, and he never seemed to give a thought about fingers that might get smashed.

* * *

Some days in that summer of 1981 Irene would get Reba's blue-haired Aunt Gladys to stay around the house and fix lunch for Carolee while she and Royce crisscrossed the piney woods and sand flats, scouting the country in his Olds Super 88. Between them on the seat lay a briefcase with leather straps loose across the top. Royce would drive with one hand, and with the other pull out "Tobins," landowner-ship maps made by the Tobin map company down in San Antonio. When Irene got bored she would dig out a blank oil and gas lease form (always a Texas Producers 88, which for some time she thought had a strange relationship to Royce's car) with two pages of tiny print and study it. She would read it aloud, the cold blast from the a/c zipping through the Olds, whipping the document while she stumbled over hydrocarbons and puzzled over shut-in provisions. Then for miles she listened to Royce try to unpuzzle things.

Irene and Royce stopped in a crossroads store at noon for lunch—a hunk of rat-trap cheese and saltines and a couple of cans of Vienna sausages. In the cool darkness of that store they balanced on end-up Coke cases while Royce divided the cheese and speared sausages with his pocketknife. He sorted them half and half on the butcher paper between them. Within easy reach two Dr Peppers wept circles on the plank floor.

Three or four men sank quiet into one corner, eyes stuck on a cold wood stove, and for a while Royce and Irene ate in silence, listening to a chair creak, or a squirt of tobacco juice as it hit the bottom of a coffee can. But after a bit, as if he were onstage and had got his cue, Royce said aloud, partly to Irene and partly to whoever would hear, "Pretty blame hot out there," and with his thumb pushed his straw hat back on his head. Everything was always "pretty blame this" or "pretty blame that," and it annoyed Irene, being too country for her taste, but she also knew that "blame" was better than Royce's other options. The fellows across the way nodded, and one said with a grunt, "Well, I'd best be going," but he didn't.

Then Royce asked about the melons turning yellow in a field back up the way and shook his head at the stalk-drooping nubbin corn they had passed in some creek bottom clearing. "Dry, but not like '57," one said. More scraping of chairs, one fellow reached around into the Coke chest and pulled out a chunk of ice and rubbed it across his forehead.

By this time Irene would be half crazy, wanting to say, for God's sake Royce, won't you just go ahead and tell them why you're here and what you're doing?

But she didn't. Instead, Irene fiddled with a thread on a button, tried to count the flattened tin cans used as floor patches, thought about what color to paint her kitchen cabinets next time, and did she really want to ask Royce if she could get a new Singer before fall, and what kind of dresses she should sew Carolee for school, and if Carolee would get her period at twelve the same way she did, and since she was almost there should she go ahead and tell her what to expect, or maybe she knew already and Irene would feel foolish later—all those thoughts almost at once and tumbling in the half-dark of that store.

And she thought of Royce with his big soft hands, and tried to recall how it felt the first time he touched the back of her neck while they danced, and how it had never felt quite that way since and how that didn't seem fair, that if it was that good once, why could it never be that way again, and she felt a vague sadness and looked at her own hands, how they were caught in a ray of light from the window and when she lifted her thumb how wrinkles bunched in little patterns on the back of her hand like they never had before, and then Royce's words, with a different pitch, urgent but not too much so, brought her back.

"Don't guess there's any oil leasing going on around here, is there?" Across the room Irene could see overalls stiffen up like they were fresh starched and hot ironed.

"Pretty quiet, I reckon," one finally said, and sure enough it got quiet again for a while.

Then Irene folded up the butcher paper, overflowing with slippery cans and rinds and crumbs inside, and with one hand twined her fingers around the empty drink bottles and moved to the door. Royce followed, like they were about to leave.

Then one of the men said, speaking to no one in particular, "Now the Bonner place, you know, back towards Payne Springs, a bunch of heirs out of Dallas. They might of let Gulf have a lease." And he went on that he couldn't swear to it, but next thing you knew Royce had a couple of them pointing out the Bonner place on his Tobin and speculating who else might and might not be willing to lease.

Irene passed the time looking at rolls of oilcloth and then wandered outside, enjoying the shade of a red oak tree and the rhythm of voices from inside.

"Follow the big boys, the majors," Royce told her as they pulled away from the store. "Buy right up next to them and you can't go wrong."

And for a while he didn't. He'd locate a hundred acres open next to where an oil company was taking a block and pay for it with a thirty-day draft to give him time to "check the title." By doing this Royce could operate without ever putting up any cash of his own. The danger always present was that if you couldn't move the lease before the thirty days ran out and had to let the draft go back unpaid, word would get around the county. Then you had to either trade on a cash-only basis—an impossibility for someone like Royce—or you'd be flat out of the business. But so far it had worked, and Royce would take off to Houston or Fort Worth to sell the leases, and with a little luck and a lot of pushing he'd roll back into town with double his money.

Late that summer and acting on a tip, Royce managed to tie up some leases out north of town almost offsetting a deep test that Gulf had staked a few weeks before. He told Irene that this was the break he had been waiting for, and to celebrate he took her over to the County Line for their all-the-ribs-you-can-eat night, and the next morning Royce took off for Houston with a briefcase stuffed with leases.

Two days later the local paper announced that the well was dry, that Gulf had plugged and abandoned it. Royce stayed gone for three weeks, calling home with word first that Gulf had claimed a dry hole to force him out of the area, and then a week later from Fort Worth telling Irene not to worry, he'd be home with a tub full of cash before she knew it.

On Irene's fortieth birthday Royce called again from Oklahoma City, and the next day Mr. Collins from the Dixie Drugstore delivered a Whitman's Sampler to the house. Irene tossed the box on the dining room table they never used and for three days it remained there, untouched and unacknowledged by Irene. One day the box was gone and Irene figured that Carolee and her friends couldn't stand it any longer.

After that Royce stayed on the go a lot. When he came home he'd glance at the stacks of messages by the phone and stuff them in his coat pocket. Then the messages stopped.

Some nights Royce came home late and quiet, and some nights he came home late and full of whiskey and noise. Irene let him be as much as she could, knowing as she did that some things a man had to work out for himself.

But Irene told herself not to be a fool, that men did leave their wives. They died or were killed, this she knew, or they ran off with other, mostly younger women. Reba recommended a new (for her) up-the-side-and-teased-in-the-back hairdo and spoke of Royce with uncharacteristic reverence, adding that a good man is hard to find and a bird in the hand and so on until Irene thought she would scream before she could get installed under the dryer, but she didn't.

Irene knew that Royce might leave, might have to in order to get a job. She knew women in that very town who had
been left, most not all at once in a sudden night but gradu-
ally, their men taking jobs "temporarily, just till things pick
back up around here" down at a Port Arthur refinery, sending home fifty dollars a week for a while, then everything
stopping, even the visits home. But the women for the most
part going on being Mrs. Frank Ramsey or Mrs. Red
Larkin, clerking at the dime store or working the office at
the cattle auction two days a week. The women's eyes always going in two directions, hoping to catch a sign from
somewhere that Frank or Red would truly and forever be
coming back, and simultaneously watching for that remote
possibility that another man who might be snared would
wander by.

Another man. As a young woman Irene would have found
unthinkable even the possibility of ever having two husbands in her life. But now, as Royce's stays out of town got
longer and longer, she had to wonder. Would she want
there to be a second? Irene said no, emphatically no, but still
couldn't help but think that possibility might slip into her
future as smoothly as Royce seemed to be slipping into her
past. Oh, the past seemed to happen so fast these days.

She remembered, as a teenager, watching twice-married
women in town as they pushed carts through Piggly Wig-
gly's, or in Penney's pulling sundresses off the rack and
holding them up, studying a mirror with quizzical looks on
their faces. Irene remembered thinking, watching those
women's faces, that they had known, had lain naked and
done all sorts of the most private acts with, not only one
man but two, or even more, and how their faces showed
nothing of the turmoil, the gyrations produced by moving
casually, it seemed, in and out of strange beds, their faces
after all that as plain and ordinary as pound cake.

And now Irene understood. For the first man melts coldly
away like a long-ago-lit candle and you go on with what is

yours and what is now. The past forgotten and the future out there unformed, waiting to surprise you like a three-block-away float in a parade.

Irene knew this could happen, that she could be one of those women left slumped in their empty rooms, but knew also that Royce wouldn't leave for some refinery job or some new-to-town sparkly-toed floozy. If Royce left it would be for something that Irene realized she could never really know. Some dark part of Royce that all men seemed to have, but for Royce had been portioned out in a bigger dose.

Whatever it was, Irene had tried and for the most part failed to figure out, even in her best thinking times bent over the ironing board or with full sink suds up to her Sunday elbows. Whatever it was could banish—banish was exactly the right word—a man from his territory in defeat and shame and he would never be the same, or at least never show his face again.

If she only knew Royce better, she thought, and laughed at how crazy that sounded even to herself. Maybe if she had known him as a boy, had sat behind him in school and watched him do something, maybe learn to write, something that simple. Had watched him carefully, the awkward way he held a pen, the way he struggled with something that was basic and free of bluster and bluff, so that the scratching on paper proved effort and skill and could be seen and understood and figured out. And Irene would have rescued one of those crumpled and discarded papers for herself, and today, as Royce's wife, she could smooth out the wrinkles and see back to what he had been. Who he was.

When Royce was home Irene wanted to talk to him about his work, the way it had dried up to nothing, and how did he think that pile of bills stuffed under the phone book would go away. But she'd no more than bring it up and the next thing she knew Royce was out in his Olds, studying a map or something for a long time.

Irene knew he kept a bottle of bourbon somewhere, probably under the seat of the Olds, for that's where he spent most of his time. She could smell it through his Listerine breath.

Irene kept trying to figure out what she should be for Royce, and made a list of words that came to mind. Steady, constant, loyal, supportive, strong, gentle. She wrote obedient and scratched through it. She read a *Reader's Digest* article, "Out of Work, Out of Hope? No!" and one in a *Ladies Home Journal*, "Bad Times for a Good Man—What *You* Can Do."

But this was different, she knew. Royce wasn't your ordinary out-of-work man, someone laid off in a steel mill strike or bumped off an assembly line. He had pride and talent and . . . and then it came to Irene that Royce had never trained himself to do anything but sell—himself or leases or whatever else, it didn't matter. Maybe he had sold her, too, and she had fallen for it.

The world would finally catch up with Royce, see right through him, and it wouldn't take Superman X-ray eyes, either. Even Irene would see through Royce. Even his own wife. Then she told herself to stop imagining the worst. She was bad about that, she knew, even Royce had told her so— how many times? Called her Miss Gloomy when she got worried about Carolee or how old the roof was, or how three boys she had gone to high school with had died already (one after twelve years crippled with polio, one in a Butane truck wreck, and one tangled all night in a trotline he'd stretched across the Trinity River after a flood). All the worry was foolish, she knew, and besides that a waste of time.

One regular Thursday morning at Reba's Irene couldn't help herself, going on and on, being Miss Gloomy for sure. Finally, Ruby stopped her, poking her shoulder with a curler. "Irene," she said, "all you need is what Ruby's had all along. A job. Doesn't have to be a good one. Look at this." And she laughed and swung her arm around the beat-up old beauty parlor. "But you need somewhere to get dressed up and go. A place away from Royce. In fact, a place away from men in general."

Irene sat up and wiped a soap bubble from her eye. "Ruby," she said, "I've never worked a day in my life outside the house. What in the world could I do? Especially here, in a place as dead as Five Oaks."

"Go with what you know," Reba said. "Just look at the way you sew, the nice way you dress."

Irene looked at her skirt, the hem crease still showing where she had let it down last year. She shook her head.

"Just think about it," Reba said. "Just think about it." Reba patted her on the shoulder and talked her into a half-price permanent, saying it was a new, improved formula that the supplier was pushing, and "just what a working woman needs."

It was too easy. Nina's Ready-to-Wear was the only dress shop in town, and Nina was bored with being there all day and hated alterations, so when Irene waltzed in the next morning she stayed until five o'clock to close the shop down.

Irene liked the work. It took her mind somewhere besides trying to picture Royce running here and there across the country in his Olds. The hemming and taking tucks and moving buttons in, but mostly out, came to Irene as second nature, and she lost herself in the predictable monotony of it all.

When Nina went to the bank or to lunch, however, the story was different. Those Saturday morning "customers" who took party dresses out "on approval" burned Irene the most. Come Monday morning the dresses slipped back in, sometimes splattered with God knows what, always with a Five Oaks Country Club smoky beer smell. The color was wrong they would say: "Gave me a washed-out look that you wouldn't believe" or "That style, the wide sash, you know, puts ten pounds on me, I swear." Nothing for Irene to do but steam them out the best she could, hang them out back, and hope for a stiff wind.

Five Oaks wasn't Irene's hometown. She grew up in Prospect, forty miles to the west, and although Royce laughed when she said so, that forty miles made a difference. Prospect had both a Catholic and an Episcopal church, and the people seemed more worldly and less eager to rejoice in a person's run of bad luck. Maybe being closer to Dallas, Irene thought, or maybe something in the water, made the difference. Maybe more minerals, for the land around Prospect had iron-red outcroppings that bled when it rained.

By the time the first norther blew wet and cold down through Oklahoma, the mess Royce had got into over the Gulf dry hole and all the leases he couldn't pay off had begun to settle down. The problem, he told Irene, was simple. He was just quicker than most everybody else, and if the world was always out of step with you, even a genius would have an occasional stumble.

He still avoided the Farmers and Merchants Bank and only recently had ventured a couple of times into Dixie Drug for coffee. But he had picked up a few leases, working by the day for an independent out of Dallas, and started calling Irene darlin' again.

One evening, while Irene cut up a fryer, Royce stayed on the phone a long time, then slipped out to the Olds with his calculator. When he came back in he had a big grin on his face.

"This could be big," he said. "Really big." Irene poked the knife at a pan of potatoes and didn't look up. "I'll take it slow this time, darlin', I promise, but it could be big. Really big."

Irene turned to face him. "What, if I may ask, is so really big?"

Royce got his wiser-than-all-the-world look on his face, the one Irene hated. "Sinclair's made a well out east in the county, and from what I hear, it may be a doozy. Twenty feet of shale, my source tells me, loaded with oil." He hesitated just a moment, like he was checking out the room for spies.

"I can turn twenty thousand into a hundred, just like that," and he snapped his fingers right in Irene's face.

Irene felt herself sinking, her insides falling through themselves, heavy, without hope of ever being buoyant again. She started to ask how, that twenty thousand might as well be twenty million, but Royce wouldn't let her.

"Uh-uh-uh," he said, putting his finger to her lips. "This is the answer." And he swept his arms around the room. "We'll sell the house."

Irene stood over the pan of chicken for a minute. She had just speared a crispy brown leg with her two-pronged fork and as she stood she rocked that chicken leg up and down like she was counting for an astronaut blast-off.

"This is my house," she said, her mouth tight, her eyes hard as marbles.

"Ours," Royce said.

"What?"

"It's not your house," Royce said. "It's ours."

"Well, it's *my* home."

And with that she drew the two-pronged fork back and let the chicken leg fly. The greasy spot seven feet up the wall stayed there for weeks.

Then she had what she later described to Reba as a full-blown hissy-fit, potholders and flour and chicken going everywhere.

Royce left her there screaming. As he raced out the door he yelled back to a frightened Carolee that he had to go check on a deal.

The Olds was still gone the next morning and Irene knew she had got just what she deserved, exactly what, with a whole run of bad judgment, she had set herself up for.

Royce did come back, but nothing was the same. At supper he would sit there in silence, not touching his food, gravy glazing over on his plate. Finally he would say, "We do have butter, don't we." But Irene couldn't make herself move, not even to the refrigerator for butter. Irene knew exactly what was bound to happen, but couldn't force herself to act to stop it.

She stared icicles at her plate, poor Carolee hopping here and there, trying to be the peacemaker, fetching this and that, finally becoming hopelessly quiet.

The next week Royce told Irene that Mississippi was having a boom that wouldn't wait, there was big money to be made, and for sure he couldn't make that kind of money around here without some capital. He waited a moment for her reply.

"Anything you want," she said firmly, "but not my house." Royce nodded, said he would be back.

She hardly noticed him gone at first and to be truthful felt a sense of relief, at least for a few days.

Royce called Irene from Jackson every week or so, and mailed an occasional check. The checks didn't comfort Irene, although she deposited them the same day, knowing that she might be becoming one of those long-distance wives common to the town. With the last check Royce had scribbled a note: "Things are falling my way now. Plan to move out as soon as Carolee's school is out." Irene left the note out on her dresser where she could study its message for a few days, which ran on to be a few weeks.

One rain-soaked Tuesday in April, while Carolee was still at school, Irene started to call Royce at the number he had given her for emergencies. But she knew she would get some hotel clerk who would complain about taking calls unless it was a true emergency. And is it, he would ask? Well, not really, she would say, but well, yes, in a way it is, but no, no one has died exactly, I mean no one has died at all, not really, no, not in the hospital either, and yes, I know I could leave a number, but can't you just check his room to see, or send someone there, maybe a bell boy . . . it's the third floor and you say the elevator—okay, just forget it. Irene didn't want Royce to get a message from her, not one that said please call, and for that to be the only reason—*please call*—and she would have to wait and rehearse exactly what she would say and he might call when she was in town and he would tell Carolee his plans before she could tell him, tell him . . . what?

On the other hand a change, as she thought more about it, might do both her and Carolee some good. Five Oaks *could* be a trashy little town at times and Nina, despite her good intentions, had shown her colors as a small-town snob. Now with Irene coming in five days a week, Nina had of all things taken up golf and hung out more at the country club than at the shop and would Irene really even *want* to be a partner with her?

And the Reba Bells of the world are a dime a dozen, not that she hasn't been a good and loyal friend, but Irene might as well face it, Reba is now and always will be a gossip. And she probably couldn't even land a beauty operator's job in Jackson or Hattiesburg, not to mention Biloxi.

Irene then found herself doing something strange, but something she had seen Royce do dozens of times when he was worried. She took a Coke from the refrigerator and went out to the driveway and settled herself behind the wheel of her Ford. She sipped the Coke awhile, then rested it on the dash and closed her eyes. She tried to relax to see what would happen, but nothing much did. After a while she conjured up an image of Royce, but he had a cocky look on his face she didn't like, so she switched to Reba and then Nina, finally moving quickly on to Carolee.

Nothing worked. She might as well have been flipping through some old picture album for all the good this was doing. Then suddenly an image began to form somewhere far back behind her eyes. It was fuzzy at first, but pretty quickly Irene saw that it was of herself, and the image grew, soon taking over her whole mind.

One instant she was in her kitchen talking to Carolee, and then she was at Nina's and the next thing she knew Reba had fluffed her hair in some strange way and then she was with Royce somewhere in Mississippi, by a wide river, under a moss-dripping tree. The funny thing was, every place she pictured herself came over her with a soft feeling, one of contentment.

Then she thought she knew how Royce must have felt all those times alone in the Olds, making all those decisions, and why he could, even being so sure of himself, make some bad ones.

She could almost hear him. Now that road right out there, he would say, will go blame near anywhere you want if you follow it long enough and don't turn off. And if a road goes somewhere you can for blame sure bet that it comes back. That's it, Irene thought. That road out there, the one that will get me to Mississippi, is the same road that will bring me back. If that's what I want, it will bring me back.

In the house Irene felt light and airy again. She moved through the front room, letting her hand glide over the back of the sofa, still puzzling at the wonder of it all. Then she moved down the hall to her daughter's room. Carolee, she said, softly at first, then louder. Carolee, honey. Help me pack a suitcase. I think it's time we were trying out Mississippi.

A High Place

THROUGH the spattered dust-mottles of the back porch screen Clinton stared out past the gray settle of the barn and down across the ragged hay meadow. He sadly shook his head. Bitterweeds and goatweeds and bull nettles sprang up here and there, taking over the field in defiant clumps. When Ramiro got back from town Clinton just might jump-start the tractor and clip the tops one last time with the bush-hog. But most of the year had already slipped by and mowing weeds in November, he knew, would only scatter the ripened heads. Clinton sank a little, then tried to welter himself up by deep-poking his old weed-hating anger, but he hardly felt a stir. He pushed the screen door open with his foot and spit. It was too late for him, his pasture-mowing days were over.

Clinton had sent Ramiro into town to pick up a special order from the lumberyard, long-leaf pine, one-by-sixes and one-by-tens, freighted in all the way from somewhere on

the Pacific coast. It was already ten-thirty and Clinton wondered if Ramiro was going to take all day. Maybe the Mexican had a woman, or had been baited into a midmorning
poker game. Clinton laughed to himself. No, he's like me,
too damned old for that nonsense anymore. Maybe Ramiro
was just wandering around town in the same way that Clinton wandered around his farm, killing time, not sure what
he was waiting for, but for damned sure in no hurry to stir
the day along.

Clinton stepped out into the yard. He tried to keep his
breathing shallow so as not to start up the pain again, and
McGee sidled up to him. She left a smear of black cat fur on
his khaki pants and spent a long minute polishing the tops of
his boots with her chin.

With his foot he pushed her gently to one side and moved
toward the barn, the cat right behind. A big-as-your-thumb
grasshopper hit against his shirt and clung there halfheart-
edly. Midsummer and they nearly knock you down, but let
the first norther whistle down through the Panhandle and
they seem to give up, knowing that it's all nearly over.
Clinton brushed the grasshopper off and McGee pounced
quickly, happy to start the morning with a little game of ver-
min torture.

Clinton leaned against the east side of the barn, letting
the warmth of the sun soak into his bones. From there he
could just hear the semis gear down, slowing, and then with
a strain grind their way fiercely up the on-ramp and onto the
interstate. A noise he had never got used to.

A pair of hawks glided overhead, drawing smooth loops
in the hazy air. McGee, the one-legged grasshopper still
twitching in her mouth, cowered when a shadow swept
across the grass.

"You better keep your eye on them suckers," Clinton told
McGee, and nodded, agreeing with himself, for he knew
there would be more. In November you could always see a
high spew of hawks moving in slow circles toward Mexico.

From above McGee would stand out as a tasty black and white snack.

One November before, so many years back, the field below dotted with a scattering of brindled cows, Clinton had lain hidden with his daddy among the tall tufts of grama and love grass and waited for the hawks. The grass was the same as now, he could still see it in his mind, the green faded with the first frost, but still upright and rippling across the hill like an ivory ocean.

McGee took the lead as Clinton hobbled down the slope from the barn and moved toward the field. He passed through the shadows of a narrow grove of bois d'arcs, stepping around horseapples half-sunk thick and fetid in the bare ground. At the far edge of the trees he stood for a minute, breathing heavily in the shade until the cool began to creep in. Then he wandered out into the waving grass.

After a few minutes he spotted a small rise thick with knee-high patches of love grass and made his way there. He stood quiet and heavy for a moment, then turned slowly, stopping long enough to gaze in each direction. Overnight, it seemed, his neighbor's field to the south had turned green with a fine thatch of winter rye. Clinton knew that green field might be the last he would ever see, the warm showers of next spring stretching too far away even for him to dream.

The hills to the west loomed rough and shadowed and scabbed, speckled with the white of limestone outcroppings and scrub bush. They hovered above the creek bottom that meandered a deep cut through his place.

Clinton toed the sandy loam where he stood and was satisfied with the easy way it gave. Then he murmured aloud, "This just might be the place," and with some effort let himself down to a sitting position, finally lying back into the thin softness of the grass. The long Z of stitches across his belly pulled and he had a hard time letting himself go enough to fully extend. McGee circled him once and then crawled onto his chest. She kneaded his softness, her nose almost at his chin. Clinton crossed his arms to protect his tender stomach and let her be.

High clouds washed out the blue above him. He closed his eyes. It seemed as if he had lain in that field with the stubble pushing at his back only the week before. But it had been more than seventy years. He breathed deeply. Everything seemed the same—the sour yet fragrant mustiness of the grass, the dry ticking of leaves that wickered the barbwire fence—only the faint hum from the interstate was new. That and, of course, Clinton no longer being a boy. He had lived until he was old—he hated to say the word but it was so true—old with a knot of never-to-go-away pain in his stomach.

When he was five or six Clinton had stretched out with his daddy in that same November field while the ancestors of these same hawks swept circles above. No talking, no moving, his father had whispered, and young Clinton steeled himself, determined not to so much as twitch. They waited for the moment when a curious hawk would glide over, dropping lower and lower, finally looming directly above them, almost filling the sky.

Clinton quickly had taught himself how to remain still, how to ignore the grass and bugs and weeds and trees. He learned to concentrate on the sky above him, looking out beyond the clouds, straining his eyes and stretching his mind in an attempt to see as far as he could, taking himself farther and farther into the universe above him. Those times in the field with his daddy it stopped right there, and he would lose himself in a silence that only he could know.

But there were other times. When he was alone, when things were right, he could push himself so far out into space that at the moment of his last imagined glimpse of the nothing that was there his mind would finally short circuit. He both loved and feared coming to that moment, for it always sparked a sudden dizziness, one that caused him in panic to throw out his arms and grab the clumps of grass around him so as not to fall forever off the earth and into some endless void. At that moment, when the immensity of everything finally overwhelmed him and he was emptied of all understanding, a little shudder would stir through him. Not a convulsive shudder as from fear or cold but a pleasurable shudder, one not totally unlike the convulsion he later would find in sexual release.

It was an orgasm of sorts, he later guessed, not bound to the groin, but one that tingled through his entire body. He figured it was an attempt to grasp infinity before he even knew the word or had ever seen and puzzled over that endlessly curving symbol.

Then his daddy would half-rise, jolting young Clinton back to the sting of the weeds at his back. The earth shook with the blast of a single shot from the gun, quickly followed by the thud of the hawk as it hit the ground where it stayed, brown and twisted, nested in the pliant grass.

"Calf-killers," his daddy called the hawks. He told stories of half-eaten calves, their afterbirth not yet dry, their mamas snorting and bawling their helpless rage. His daddy gave a satisfied grunt as he pushed to his feet and snapped open the gun. The spent shell released with a pop and the air filled with the sweet smell of gunpowder.

Clinton carried the empty shotgun up the hill, following his daddy. He walked eye to eye with the hawk that was slung head down across his daddy's back. Clinton swayed from side to side, matching the rhythm of the lifeless bird. When his daddy slowed to jerk a particularly offensive goatweed from the ground Clinton turned back and aimed the gun, swinging it wobbly across the empty sky, feeling that he had the whole world in its sight.

Clinton heard the pickup horn give off three quick honks. Ramiro was back with the lumber. He carefully rolled to one side and pushed himself into a sitting position. From there he fell forward to get on all fours. McGee circled under his arms, wanting to play. Finally Clinton pushed himself up, but the pain jolted from him a kicked-dog yelp and McGee sprang high and to one side.

By the time Clinton worked his way back up the hill Ramiro had placed a couple of sawhorses in the sun outside the barn and had run the tangle of a cord for his circle saw. The lumber gleamed smooth-planed and yellow from the back of the truck.

Clinton watched. He liked the way Ramiro worked, the way he put his head down and didn't look up until the job was finished. Ramiro had wandered up from Mexico over thirty years ago and hung around the barn like a skinny, hungry stray. Clinton let him work for his meals and sleep in the barn, hoping that he would move on when he got a full stomach.

But that changed when Clinton saw Ramiro work. Together they laid stone walks and wormed sheep and plastered a stone smokehouse. Ramiro hoed Dora's garden and soon she trusted him to pull weeds from her flower beds. The two men framed up a little room in one corner of the barn and Ramiro stayed. At first he went back to Zacatecas every six months or so, but later just sent money orders to a sister who cared for their parents until they died. Clinton figured something had happened to Ramiro that kept him out there alone, with no family and only an occasional friend to stop by. A strange way to live, isolated like that, Clinton had thought at the time, but now with Dora gone he understood how the heart of a man could damn near rot out and leave him so empty he no longer cared where he was or how long he stayed.

Ramiro took a stick and scratched a few lines in the sand and stepped back for Clinton to see.

Clinton studied the scratches. "I don't want to be cramped," he said. "It'll be close enough in there at best. But for sure I won't need any breathing room." Both men laughed, and Clinton with a wave of his hand told Ramiro to go ahead.

When Ramiro began marking the boards and making cuts Clinton retreated to the shade of the open barn. While he watched the sawdust spin into the air he drifted here and there with his thoughts. Dora would never have gone along with this. First she would have scolded Clinton and then spoiled him. She would have hid his whiskey and stirred up batches of potato soup; slippers in place of boots; hot salt baths instead of morning inspections down the misty hill with McGee. For sure she would have had a fit to see Ramiro building Clinton's casket.

But some things he missed. The early smell of coffee; and bacon and eggs that you fry yourself never taste the same; and biscuits—well, he'd gotten so he could hardly stand the pop when he busted a cardboard can against the counter and pulled the skinny things apart. Dora's biscuits had been big as a tomcat's head.

And as annoyed as he had got at Dora second-guessing all the TV stories, her voice *had* warmed and filled the house.

And the bed somehow seemed smaller now instead of larger like it should have. Some nights he nearly fell off one side and then the other.

And he did snore, could even hear himself, but couldn't wake enough to stop without Dora there to push him onto his side.

As it had worked out, with Dora already two years gone, Ramiro had brought him home from the hospital. Clinton downed bowls of *posole* and *menudo* and sipped *mescal* diluted with the juice of Mexican limes. He was back in his boots in no time at all.

When Clinton told Ramiro about the operation, that it had been no more than a quick survey of his insides followed by a sad shake of the doctor's head and a nice stitch job, the Mexican just nodded, as if to say, yes, I understand, your time to die has come. Then, with a little shrug, Ramiro said,

"I will help you to live while you can and help you to die when you must." Like dying was no great event at all. Or maybe it was such a great event that it had been expected always, almost to the point of being welcome when it finally came. As if to die is out of your hands, a little sad, but only a little if you have lived a long life, and for sure should be no surprise. And to have the time and wherewithal to supervise the building of your own casket, especially from seasoned boards of long-leafed pine—that was a double blessing.

Ramiro drilled the boards and secured them with brass screws. He sanded the dovetails of the tight joints smooth. In the afternoon, while Clinton dozed in the daybed on the porch, Ramiro waxed and buffed the box until it shone.

The next morning Clinton woke early. He boiled coffee by the pink half-light of the sky and sat on the porch waiting for Ramiro to stir. Other years he would have spent the day shelling corn or winterizing the tractor or going into town to check the price of alfalfa hay. Dora had practically pushed him out of the house those hard-bit winter days and he would have spent mornings warming around the "bull ring" at Boyd's Cafe, mostly stirring one last cup of coffee and trading insights on the local football prospects and complaining about the Cowboys. But the boys there had thinned out so that Clinton no longer had the heart to stop by. Too many ghosts at the table.

When Ramiro had gathered his tools—grubbing hoe, sharpshooter, and round-bladed shovel—Clinton stepped out into the yard. A crisp norther had swept across the hill country in the night and the air had freshened; the sky soared pale and blue forever.

Ramiro wheelbarrowed the tools down the hill. McGee scampered alongside and Clinton followed behind. Ramiro stopped at the edge of the bois d'arc thicket only long enough for Clinton to catch up and point out the rise of high ground that he had chosen.

Ramiro tested the earth with the sharpshooter and nodded. He looked around as if to orient himself, and Clinton could read his mind. "Run it this way," Clinton said with a wave of his hand. "East and west." And without another word Ramiro began to dig Clinton's grave.

Dora had chosen a place next to her mother in the town cemetery. But it had gotten too newfangled for Clinton. The add-on part was all golf-course grass and wads of plastic flowers with not a single upright marble stone. A brass-plated country club for the dead, he called it. "Just as soon be buried out front of the Safeway as there," he told Ramiro.

When Ramiro was knee-deep in the earthen rectangle he stopped. The last few shovelsful had been caliche. He reached over and crumbled some of the gritty white clay in his hand.

"How deep you want me to go?"

Clinton thought a minute. He felt himself wondering about the whole idea as the grave had begun to take shape.

"It doesn't matter," Ramiro said, "I can go as deep as you want." He stepped up out of the hole and McGee leaped in to take his place. "But for this caliche I must have the pinch bar, and water, too." He kicked at the caliche as if it were alive. "It will not be easy now," he said and quickly moved up the hill towards the barn.

Clinton moved slowly around his half-dug grave. He knew how deep he wanted it, he could have told Ramiro right away to get a foot deeper than a coyote could dig. He figured three, three-and-a-half feet should do it. Didn't want coyotes messing him up more than what all the years had already done. Didn't want a gathering of turkey buzzards hovering around either.

But that wasn't the main problem. Clinton moved to the grassy side of the hole. He knelt for a minute, thinking, then with some difficulty stretched out on his back beside the grave. He reached one hand over and ran his fingers down the cold exposed earth as far as he could. When he stopped

McGee batted at them twice and then raced up and out of the grave.

To Clinton the earth had always seemed warm and friendly, in season nurturing potatoes and onions and beans and bringing forth fields of long-stemmed grass for his cattle. Now all he could feel was the cold. And then he imagined the weight. All the caliche tossed back on top. And the dark. My God the dark and the cold. The loneliness of it all.

Maybe the doctor had been wrong. Maybe it's only a cranky appendix or something. Maybe gallstones. They can cause pain like that, he'd heard. Maybe. Maybe he'd be the first one not to play the game to the usual end. Just because everybody else had died didn't mean he had to. What would Ramiro do with him gone? And his first not-yet-quite-born great-grandchild? Forced to grow up in California, of all places, would in all likelihood need him to help, sooner or later. It wasn't fair. Just about the time you get things all figured out, when you're finally in shape to live a somewhat decent life, the damned whistle blows and it's all over.

The wind picked up just a little and once again Clinton could hear the dry scratch of leaves on the fence. A couple of hawks had spotted him and McGee; they glided in a tight circle.

Then Clinton took a breath, as deep as he dared, and let himself go. His eye went from a stalk of love grass that waved next to his face, and then up to the tree line at the fence and on past the hawks. The morning moon lay pale against the washed-out sky. There were stars after that, although he could not see them. And planets, and other stars and galaxies, and his mind stretched, trying to move out past them all. Then he got to the edge again, a place where there were no stars and no moons and no planets and the emptiness washed over him again. And then he felt himself falling. Instinctively he reached out to catch himself, one hand finding a clump of grass and his other hand dangling into the emptiness of the half-dug grave. A slight tremor went through him. He felt the little shudder once again. And again it gave him pleasure, but this time of a different sort. It gave him comfort in a way he'd never known.

Ramiro's shadow fell across him. "You are all right?" he asked. Clinton looked up and nodded. He rolled over onto all fours and then sat back in the grass.

"I want it deep, Ramiro," he said. He thought of his great-grandchild, maybe just a few months from now, being carried around the yard up there, being told that this is the house that your great-grandfather built, and these are his cows, and this is McGee, Great-Granddaddy Clinton's cat.

"I want it deep, and then when it's all over I want it mounded high. Cover it with a pickup load of those limestone rocks from the hills," he said. "Paint my name on one of 'em. Don't want no plastic flowers, no fancy marker. But I want it deep and I want those rocks stacked high so that you can see it from the house. That's all."

Photo by Lynn Watt

D ONLEY WATT has lived in Texas most of his life. He has worked as a landman in the oil business, owned an herb farm, and been the dean of a community college, among other things. He is the author of a novel, *The Journey of Hector Rabinal*, and his stories have appeared in various literary journals. He and his artist wife, Lynn, now live in Tucson.